A note from the author

When I was very young, I spent time on a farm.
The farm was down a leafy lane which was quiet and green and wobbly, with a mid-bank of grass. It had ruts and hollows; my wellies sploshed in the muddy puddles.
I talked to cows, munching their breakfast. They let me stroke their wet noses and licked my hands with great, long tongues.
I climbed stiles to stare at the hedgerow cobwebs in the morning dew. I touched thistles, hawthorn and holly.
I saw mushrooms, and moss clinging to tree trunks.
I watched crows, hearing them crauk-crauking overhead.
It took me a long time to walk down that lane.
I was always late.
But I didn't care.

www.rachaellindsay.com

Also by the same author

The Warrior Troll

The Bogler's Apprentice

Of Pipes and Potions

The Quest of Snorrie Magnus

Stolen Secrets

Tales From The Dark Hole:
The Changeling's Child

Rachael Lindsay

Tales From The Dark Hole:

The Changeling's Child

Nightingale Books

A CIP catalogue record for this title is
available from the British Library.

ISBN 978 190 755 287 8

Nightingale Books is an imprint of
Pegasus Elliot MacKenzie Publishers Ltd.
www.pegasuspublishers.com

First Published in 2016

Nightingale Books
Sheraton House Castle Park
Cambridge England

Printed & Bound in Great Britain by CMP (uk) Limited

Dedication

For my baby-pie, kipperling, grandson

Seth Jay,

with all Oma's love

xx

Acknowledgement

My special thanks and deep love to
Natalie Fern
for her imagination and creativity.

I know that this story, with these characters, has always
had a special place in her heart.
My words have been brought to life, beautifully.

natalie.fern1@gmail.com

Preamble

The way through the forest is deep and dark.

The Leaf Man watches.

The Leaf Man waits.

The Leaf Man listens...

    Drip.

        Drop.

            Dribble.

                Drobble.

He knows she will come.

The long, green, slime fronds are a shifting curtain of secrecy. They droop limpidly over the eerie, hideaway place beneath. The air is heavy, moist and silent, apart from the steady drip,

        drop,

            dribble,

                drobble,

falling through the dinge. Fleetingly, a shaft of light pierces the mist, striking Great Boulder as if to lance the blemishes and knobbles on its surface, but then the long, green, slime fronds suck together and cut the single beam out.

All is still once more in the deep, clammy gloaming.

There are no flowers here and few creatures dare to venture near this lonely retreat, least of all the trolls, who prefer the fresh air and sunshine moments of other forest parts. Only the ignorant, or the foolhardy, or those who have lost their way, would come here – and for good reason.

Apart from one.

The Leaf Man sees her footprints in the moss carpet and knows this is the way she has walked. The Leaf Man waits for his minions to report back to him.

What has been her business?

He listens, ready to make mischief under the

      drip,

            drop,

                  dribble,

                        drobble

of the long, green, slime fronds, for he knows that sorcery hangs in the air. There is a pungent odour of enchantment that most would find overwhelming.

Suffocating.

Especially at the Witching Hour.

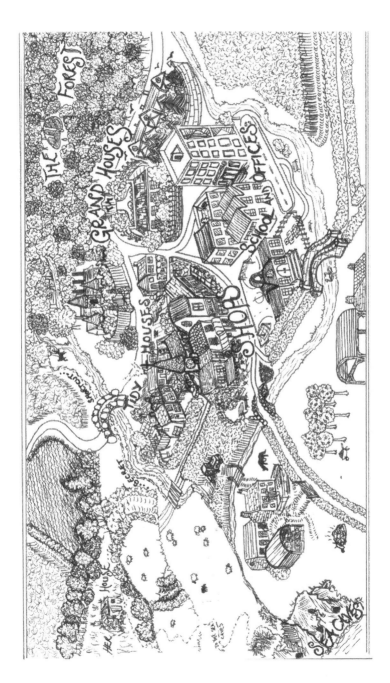

Chapter One

I f you walk towards the setting sun, nestling in its bed of evening cloud, you will leave the forest behind. The air becomes less oppressive and the sky opens above your head. You will pass the grand houses; the ones with long driveways and fancy names: Moss Towers, Ravens' Hall and Ivy Turrets. You will be able to steal a glimpse of life, though only if you jump to peep over the perimeter walls, or find a gap to spy through, in the dense prickles of the guardian hedges. These gates are always padlocked against the world.

Soon, however, you will reach the town: the tidy, well-kept houses with clean paintwork and guttering, the pretty bungalows with neatly-striped lawns and flower borders of colour, the welcoming family homes, all shouting-noise, garden goalposts and Sunday-washed cars. Roads to the left and right lead to shops and schools and offices; the busy, necessary buildings of ordered, polite society.

Keep walking onwards, and you will see that the tarmac peters out eventually. The road surface becomes peppered with pot-holes and increasingly loses any formal line. Cars, buses and the bustling hum of everyday goings-on are left behind, and ahead of you is a simple lane. It is a rather wobbly lane, twisting and turning, with ruts and hollows which collect rainwater, forming muddy, wellie-splashing opportunities. Should you have time to continue your exploration this day – or any other – whether walking idly, freewheeling on your bike, or trotting your horse, the lane roughens into an old, disused farm track. The ruts and hollows now give way to well-worn, dug-in grooves and a risen mid-bank of grass. The hedgerows are wild here, growing in a tangle of nettles and bramble. Thistles spike their way through hawthorn and holly. Secret nests fall silent as you approach and hedgehogs curl tightly into fallen leaves, waiting for the tremor of your feet to pass. The trees on either side are aged, bowed in greeting, forming an arbour which tunnels the lane away into the distance.

There is little point taking your wellies, bicycle wheels or horse's hooves any further. All that lies at the bottom of the lane, is *her* home. You *might* creep closer. As a dare. Curiosity *might* just get the better of you.

Gaggles of girls and tribes of boys have, on occasion, tiptoed nearer, hearts racing, legs trembling, but – twitchy as squirrels – they have pelted back home at the slightest sign of movement from within, screaming and yelling in frightened, skittish excitement.

The weather-beaten farm cottage used to belong to a shepherd, many years ago. It was a warm, snug home, then. Not any more though. The shepherd has long since departed.

Now it is *her* home.

Now, some bricks lie in piles where there used to be walls. The ruins are largely open to the elements; the windows are no longer glazed and torn remnants of tatty curtains flap in the breeze, offering little respite from the weather. Jackdaws, rooks and crows swoop on glossy, black wings from their nests in high tree tops, to circle the tumbledown chimney.

Crauk! Crauk! Crauk!

Clinging tendrils of ivy clutch their way up the ancient stones, with sticky tentacles winding around the crumbling stack. Long ago, a dropped seed fell through the open roof and onto a patch of mud in between the broken floor slates. The resulting sapling forced itself ever upwards, growing mature in the centre of the cottage, twisting branches through gaps in the dilapidated walls, stretching and grasping, gnarled fingers at the sky. Roots, like writhing snakes, began to invade the floor, spreading to reach all corners. One stormy night, a bolt of lightning had blackened this tree, but the charred form still stood strong; as much a part of the house now, as the bricks and stones.

However, although derelict, if you dared to get close enough to peer inside, you would see signs of life: the recent ashes of a fire in the hearth with mugwort laid over to keep it smouldering; the dried tansy, rosemary and burr marigold tied tightly and hanging from the knotted beam; the cellar door not swinging open on useless hinges, but bolted shut against unwelcome intruders; a bent bicycle, with a battered basket and a rusty bell, leaning against one wall and a few chickens peck-pecking their way through the rubble.

If all is quiet, it is because the occupant is not at home. She is busy elsewhere.

"Come now, you two! The time is sun-dialling fast and soon the dimsk will be upon us. We must quick-hurry to beat it."

Warty Toad and Snidey Slug glanced up through the long, green, slime fronds at the gathering gloom. It was difficult to make progress through the squelching moss and mud, but they did not wish to be in this deepest part of the forest during night hours, so they gathered their strength and hurried as best they could. The toad plopped soggily from stone to stone, sometimes slipping in the wet, sometimes resting to look above and below. He hated the damp conditions and would have much preferred drier terrain. The slug chose to slither his way between and around the stones, eye-stalks waving, constantly searching. Their mistress would not be happy if they returned home empty-handed.

"Is you keeping your eyes sharp? Is you sniffling out? Is you alerting your ears?" they were asked, as they traipsed along. "Remember searchings make findings, my Dear Ones. Searchings make findings!"

The two pets accompanied and assisted on outings such as this, every few days. The trek always led them away from the ramshackle cottage, skirting via a rickety stile and short cut, along the back of the houses of the town, hidden behind hedgerows and undergrowth, to the forest. Within a few minutes they would be lost in the dinge, veiled beneath the long, green, slime fronds which dripped and

dropped and

dribbled and

drobbled onto their heads.

They were safe from prying eyes of the townspeople here, secreted away from their nosy curiosity. They were free to go about their collecting business exactly as they wished, as long as they kept as quiet as possible. None of them had any desire to be seen, or heard. They did not want the trouble it would bring.

This, the Leaf Man knew. He too, was hidden from view.

It was Snidey Slug who made the first finding, of course. It always was, and Warty Toad sighed inwardly. He was resigned now to the preening and self-congratulation that would follow. The fat slug was delighted with himself as he came to an abrupt halt and made an excited squeak. Their mistress stopped in her tracks and twizzled around in the mud, scraping it between her boots to form a circle. She bent double towards the ground, nose and chin almost touching; her one, working eye screwed up.

"What is it your searchings is delivering, Snidey?" she whispered, her breath steaming slightly.

A half-slither forwards and a nudge of a blunt nose revealed the finding.

There it lay, shining, in the moss. The claw of a songbird's foot.

"A-ha!" Her exclamation punctured the air and with a deft flick of a hooked, grimy fingernail, the tiny object was scooped up and held aloft, between finger and thumb. "A flying creature's talon," she murmured. "You *is* doing well, Snidey Slug. You *is* doing well, my love."

The slug drew himself up with pride and crooned at his mistress, who he adored. Her words of praise made him swell with happiness and he closed his tentacle eyes, all the better to savour the moment. He felt so important. He felt so very smug. He felt so *special!*

Warty Toad felt sick. Wasn't it always the way?

"It's only because you are much closer to the ground, slug," he grumbled through the side of his mouth, which otherwise was sulking and pouty. "It's not that you are better at finding stuff, you know."

Snidey Slug gave no reply. It would have been beneath him to do so and he was basking in the glow of being the Favourite One.

"I *will* eat you, one day, you know," Warty Toad threatened. "Just watch your back."

This was a threat often repeated and, as always, Snidey Slug took no notice. He knew that Warty Toad would never risk the wrath of their mistress. In silence, the two continued on their way through the slime and sludge, each searching to score against the other. The songbird's claw had been carefully examined to check for any imperfection, and finding none, it had been dropped into an overcoat pocket for safe-keeping.

"Your turn best be next happening," Warty Toad was told, somewhat sharply. The toad gulped and looked more than a little concerned.

There was a rippling of moss, quiet and delicate. The Mexican hand wave beneath their feet was almost indiscernible as the minuscule strands bent over, ever so slightly, passing a message on.

However, it was neither Warty Toad, nor Snidey Slug, who found the next treasure. The squelching, slurping and sliding of their journey came to a sudden stop, at a swift signal from their mistress.

The finding was well out of their reach and took skill and an experienced hand to snatch it. Dexterity and a keen eye were needed; the two pets had neither of these. Above their heads was a small gap in the long, green, slime fronds. The last rays of the sun made them blink as they looked upwards. Warty Toad and Snidey Slug were instructed to remain perfectly still, as black eye searched and nostrils flared, the scent of prey being inhaled deeply.

Sniff, sniff. Sniff, sniff.

Silence.

Sniff, sniff. Sniff, sniff.

Arms outstretched at either side, *twelve* distorted fingers spread in anticipation; mouth clamped tight shut.

Sniff, sniff. Sniff, sniff.

Warty Toad and Snidey Slug held their breath, every muscle in their bodies, taut, anxious expectancy etched on their faces. What was it, she had found? Whatever could it be?

It was just when Snidey Slug was about to draw a desperate, thin breath through pursed lips – and just when Warty Toad was about to pass out, and was considering whether it would be noisier to breathe suddenly, or fall dead off the rock – that one of those outstretched arms punched up through the gap and made a *snatch!* She withdrew from the light, quickly, causing the long, green, slime fronds to glide and ripple together letting a shower of droplets fall onto the moss and mud, quite drenching her two companions. Her fist was clenched tightly over her prize. A slow smile spread wickedly across her face and the green dinge glowed yellow as her good eye lit up. Having recovered from their lack of air, the two Dear Ones watched her eagerly, then the closed fist was thrust down towards them.

Between her swollen, ugly knuckles were gossamer gold and turquoise pieces. So fine were they that the light from her eye shone through them, creating faint sparkles. Slowly, one-by-one, six bent fingers opened until Warty Toad and Snidey Slug could see what was in the palm of her grubby hand.

There lay – all crumpled and tattered – a large, delicate, gold and turquoise butterfly.

The poor thing's wings were bashed and battered and bruised, and it could only twitch one frail leg, pathetically.

Twitch. Twitch.

A sudden, heavy prod crushed it.

The butterfly did not move again.

Snidey Slug edged forwards. Catching the floral perfume in his nose, he sneezed violently. It was a great, wet, slimy sneeze which ruffled the flimsy, silken wings.

"Yes, my dear slug. She is smelling of prettiness and flowers, is she not?" The smile and glow of pleasure had vanished. "What a give-away she is being, above the long, green, slime fronds, flitting about, spreading her sickly sweetness! Free to flutter-fly and live her life, happy-smiling, not having to be hiding in nature. Oh yes! Too prettily perfect for that, she is!"

Warty Toad started to drool. 'Perfect' was certainly the word. He pressed his damp lips together in an attempt to stop the slobbering from running down his chin. He had eaten only one butterfly in his life, when he was a mere toadling, and the taste had been *out of this world!* Compared with his usual diet of gritty worms and black beetles, the flavour of butterfly was utterly heavenly. It was a great strain to see such a beautiful, big dinner in front of him and know he could not have it.

"I sees you, Warty."

The toad blinked in sudden embarrassment.

"I knows you, Warty."

The crestfallen toad lowered his chin into the moss.

"What wouldn't you be giving to get your chomping chops around *this* tasty morsel, eh?"

Warty Toad did not dare say a word in reply.

"I knows you better than you is thinking I do, dearie." The warning tone was quite clear. Then, lickety-split, the crushed butterfly was stuffed into a pocket and, with a wink of a beady eye, they continued on their way.

The Leaf Man grinned widely as he watched.

It was as the three were getting rather tired, and considering calling it a day, that Snidey Slug had a rather Nasty Experience. Warty Toad had just successfully captured two red beetles from inside a rotting log, by sucking them out through a crack in the soggy bark. It had been a real effort not to swallow them whole, because his tummy was gurgling loudly as a result of gold and turquoise butterfly thoughts, but resist temptation he did, and they were placed inside a jar, covered with a muslin cloth. He was humming a satisfied, jolly sort of toady tune, when it happened.

Snidey Slug had been slipping and slopping and slithering and slothering along, day-dreaming and crooning to himself about being a Dear One. He hadn't noticed Warty's success in red beetle finding and, more importantly, he hadn't noticed that the others had side-stepped a particularly deep slime pool. He was just re-living the glorious moment when he had spotted the songbird's claw, when – *slurrrp* – *splosh!*

In one terrible second of inattention, Snidey Slug was sinking into the depths of the pool, twisting this way and that in a vain attempt to reach the surface. He could not see which direction was up, as the green colour was so dense, and so he sank down, lower and lower, not daring to gulp for air in case he drowned. He flippered as best he could with his little, fat body but only succeeded in hurting the few puny muscles he had. He coughed and spluttered and spluttered and coughed, struggling to control his rising panic. And still he sank.

Down.

Down.

Down.

His mistress had not noticed. She was concentrating on a steeper part of the trail which was proving difficult to tread without sliding backwards. She assumed her two little pets were following, still searching for items to please her.

But Warty Toad knew. He stopped at the rock beside the slime pool and had a good think. This could be the last he would ever see of the prim, precious pet. This could be the last journey of the Slug-that-was-Smug. Ho, ho! He wouldn't be so full of himself and special now, would he? At first, this seemed a marvellous piece of good luck. He blinked his poppy eyes, smiled a warty smile and was just about to follow his mistress up the bank when he had another thought.

This might actually work *against* him though. What if she thought that he had eaten her pet? He had threatened to do so, often enough. What if she thought, that whilst her back was turned, he had actually flicked the slug into his mouth and swallowed him whole? *Gulp!* Just like that. Warty Toad shuddered; it didn't bare thinking about. The punishment of a squib from her spike, would be unbelievably awful.

Then the toad thought again. Even though swimming was not something he liked to do, if he rescued the Slug-that-Slipped, he would be the Hero-of-the-Hour! He would be praised for his loyalty, courage and daring. He would be congratulated and thanked. He would be the *truly* special Dear One!

Warty Toad hesitated no longer. With a belly flop of which all frogs would be ashamed, he launched himself into the green pool and powered his way into the depths. Within seconds he saw Snidey, who was a peculiar shade of purple, and grabbed his floppy body in his mouth. Kicking his strong back legs with determined force, the toad made his way up, up, up to the surface and spat out the pathetic pet, just as their mistress turned around.

"My dears! This is no time to be larking-fun and playful in a pool! Time and the dimsk are against us. We must hurry on our way."

Snidey Slug could make no reply. He lay, face down in the wet moss at the edge of the pool, coughing and choking. Warty Toad, anxious that his heroic act should not go unnoticed, puffed out his chest in an important manner.

"Actually, I have just saved our dear friend from drowning in this particularly nasty slime pool." He waited for a response.

There was a softening of her face and the toad was favoured with a very warm smile. Warty's eyes half drooped in pleasure at her gaze. He blushed quite pink under his warty skin.

"My dearest toad! What a wonderful companion you be, and what a true and loyal friend you is to poor Snidey Slug! Thank you for acting so swift and fastly." He was patted on the head, several times.

Snidey Slug was able to draw a deep breath at last and his colour changed from purple to grey once more. He let out a rasping wheeze which rippled through the moss as he was picked up and placed gently into a gritty overcoat pocket, alongside the jar of scuttling, red beetles and his special songbird's claw, so that he could recover completely.

"You is munching a very special teatime treat tonight, Warty," he heard his mistress whisper. "You is done well and I is thinking proudly of you."

It was the slug's turn to sulk.

At last, as dusk descended, the three reached Great Boulder. A hush fell on the little group as the toad and his mistress cast wary eyes about themselves. Snidey Slug lay perfectly still in his pocket.

"We must be hush-hush and keeping our secrets safely," Warty was reminded, as several fingernails of fresh, green slime were collected and flicked into a small pot. There were watchers and listeners in these parts. It was always wise to take care.

With a tap of a stone on its surface, Great Boulder rolled, grumbling, from its resting place, slowly revealing a Dark Hole beneath. The two dropped themselves down; one lowering herself cautiously over the edge making sure her overcoat pockets did not get squashed, the other reaching the bottom with a relieved sigh and rather a large plop. The findings were hidden quickly – a place for everything and everything in its place – before they scrambled out. Great Boulder rocked backwards and forwards again and again, until enough energy was summoned up to roll over the entrance, leaving the Dark Hole secret and hidden once more.

The mistress and her pets left the long, green slime fronds to drip and

drop and

        dribble and

                drobble.

They crept along the hedgerows and undergrowth, skirted the town, with its tidy, well-kept houses, and climbed over the rickety stile, hastily back to the ramshackle cottage. The half-broken door shut behind them with a familiar creak, as a large, black crow circled the chimney pot once and then flew off in the direction of the forest. *Crauk! Crauk!*

Chapter Two

The mugwort had kept the embers of last night's fire smouldering gently, filling the cottage with an earthy, smoky welcome. The long stems were gathered together and placed carefully in a pile in the corner so that the flames could be rekindled with a few puffs of breath and some dry straw. Warty Toad busied himself with spider-gobbling, in and around the piles of bricks. They were crunchy, bubble-popping appetisers before his very special teatime treat which had been promised, and he loved to feel the tickly wriggling on his tongue. He tried very hard to put visions of the gold and turquoise butterfly out of his head, but every time he closed his eyes to swallow, the fragrant, flimsy wings floated in front of him, making his tummy ache and his mouth water. Snidey Slug was lifted out of his pocket of safety, and placed tenderly in his favourite bed: an old, chipped teapot lid, lovingly lined with moss from under the long, green, slime fronds.

"My poor baby Dear One."

He heard the words and felt very special. In actual fact he was absolutely fine and dandy after his Nasty Experience, but he thought there was no point in looking too fit and healthy if it meant he could get some more love and attention. The slug issued a pitiful moan and, with tentacle eyes drooping, sank into his cosy, damp bed.

"My precious pet."

Warty Toad had heard enough. Jealousy rose in a hot wave as he crept over to the teapot lid. Drawing himself up to his full height, he coughed politely.

"Ahem. Ahem." He had her attention. "I suppose poor, baby, precious pet, Dear One won't be able to eat his tea today," he commented innocently. Snidey Slug opened one worried eye and pursed his grey lips. "So, as well as acting so courageously and speedily by the nasty, slime pool, I volunteer to eat Snidey Slug's tea so it won't be wasted." Warty smiled a crafty smile and closed his poppy eyes. "As another good deed for the day!"

Snidey tried to squeak out in protest, but his voice was muffled as the toad forced his face into the soft, moss pillow so he couldn't be heard.

"Your idea is being both clever *and* generous, Warty," came the response. "Good food wasted-ness is shameful and, since Snidey is so poorly feeling... You *is* thoughtfully behaving, Warty. I'm pleased-face with you!"

That worked really rather well, thought Warty Toad with smug satisfaction and released his grip to allow the slug to recover properly once more. Greedily, he tucked into his normal portion of earthworms and enjoyed his extra helping of bitter, black beetles which made up his treat for the day. Then he was given Snidey's tender leaves, dipped in a pot of mouse stew which bubbled over the fire. Bliss! He smacked his warty lips in contentment as he glanced at the sorrowful figure of Snidey Slug.

The rest of the mouse stew, complete with bones and furry bits, was finished quickly, and with cooking pot set to one side, the time was right for them to make their bed for the night. An old mattress from the local rubbish dump was pulled next to the glowing embers of the fire, and a sack, filled with farm straw, created a warm, if rather itchy, cover.

"There be's a lickings-worth of mouse stew in the pot of cookery, Snidey," the sad, little slug was told. "Is you being tempted to slip-slide inside a while?"

At last, hunger got the better of him and, needing no further encouragement, Snidey slithered as quickly as he could, to sip and lick the leftovers. He didn't care now that he looked fit and well. There was only *so* long that a slug could be attention-seeking, and he was keen to settle on the bony shoulder of their mistress for the night. Warty Toad, on the other hand, felt a little bloated after his feasting and it was all he could do to drag himself into his usual position, nestled under her hairy armpit, to digest his food. All wanted to rest after the day's searching in the forest, and the Dear Ones knew what was coming.

They had been promised a bedtime story.

"Now you is knowing me well, my Dear Ones, the time is right to tell you both something of my life-livingness so far."

Warty Toad and Snidey Slug had been waiting for this. They had been adopted and brought to the cottage a short time ago and, in appreciation of the love and care, food and shelter they received, they both assisted their mistress in any way they could. However, there were certain questions which they had not dared to ask, having been told that, when the time was right, all would be explained. To their excitement, the time, apparently, was right.

"You has counted my fingers, I'm knowing," she smiled, "and I's having twelve."

The two pets watched as twelve fingers were waggled in front of them. They both thought she had rather a lot of them.

"Twelve is better for snatching than ten, and my extras is magical electricity having."

Wow, thought Snidey Slug. Imagine having a magic, electric finger or two! Actually, he reflected, any fingers at all would be pretty good.

"And I has three eyes."

Warty Toad looked confused for a moment. He scrabbled out from beneath her damp armpit and made his way onto the sacking cover to look his mistress square in the face.

One.

Two.

He held out his stubby, toady fingers to assist with counting. He looked carefully at the grinning face before him and then back at his fingers, closing just two of them. One. Two.

"I has one *seeing* eye, so I is knowing where to go."

Warty Toad nodded.

"I has one greyed-out, blinded eye."

Warty Toad nodded again.

"The blind eye is being my eye of reason and thinking, of plotting and planning; it is helping me see things differently when problems is difficult. It is being an *inward*-seeing eye."

The toad sort of understood that, but still struggled to find the third eye.

"Eye number three is settling *inside* my forehead! I knows it is being there because I can see what others is thinking. It is helping me know their ideas and sometimes what will happen in future minutes."

Snidey Slug tried to keep up. This was all a bit strange. Twelve fingers for magic purposes and extra snatching. Then, three eyes: one to see with; one to work things out with; one to see into the future and read minds with. All in all, pretty useful, he supposed. He waved his own eye stalks and tried to imagine having an extra one of those, as well as fingers.

"And I is old. Older than anyones. I lives and lives. I sees trees grow tallsome from seedlings, standing for year after year and then I sees them crashing to the ground. I sees all people comes and goes, as time passes."

Then, their mistress seemed to fall into a half dream as she recounted her story. The two pets listened without fidgeting so that they did not miss anything.

Born countless years before, her name was Hobnail and she was never loved. Her mother despised her so much that she was not even given a name until, as a young girl, she came across a pair of discarded, old boots which just happened to fit her sore, bare feet. They were hobnail boots and since she was considered a hobgoblin in any case, a name was hers, at last: Hobnail. She was badly disfigured, born with an extra finger on each hand and a twisted spine. In addition, she was not blessed with a pretty face and was discontented and ill-tempered, arriving in the world screaming and kicking, with a ravenous appetite. Everyone around her recoiled when they saw the baby, and shunned her, immediately. Sensing she was reviled by all, her behaviour continued to be as ugly as her appearance and within days of her birth, she was labelled a changeling.

Snidey Slug had to interrupt. "Erm. S'cuse me, but what's a changeling?"

"Aah, my precious one. Changelings is coming from the faeries, so peoples thinks."

"Faeries are beautiful and kind, aren't they?"

"Not real ones, Snidey. Real ones is being nastyful, spite-creatures."

It was true that long ago, whenever a baby was born afflicted by disease or disability, people would say that this was not their *real* child. They would say that the faeries must have swapped their beautiful, healthy baby, for one of their own. It was thought that the human baby had been taken away to act as a servant to do the faeries' bidding; or sometimes that the faeries had fallen in love with the newborn; or sometimes that it was done out of spite and malice. Others thought that changelings were the offspring of sprites or elves and that the human child had gone to live with them forever. Some even maintained that the baby in their cradle was in fact an ancient faerie who had been put there to be petted and coddled by human parents, to live in comfort for the rest of its life.

Whatever the reason, people were superstitious enough to believe that any child born with something different from others, was a changeling. To avoid this dreadful situation, many years ago, mothers would put simple charms next to their babies as they slept – an open pair of scissors or a coat turned inside out – to ward off any faeries that might flit by and steal their perfect child, replacing it with one of their own. Ugly. Malformed. Hobnail was considered a changeling indeed, by her mother.

In those distant days, it was thought that if a changeling uttered an expression of surprise, its identity would be revealed and this would be proof to everyone around. No matter how young the disfigured baby was, if she were shocked, and if she really were a changeling, she would cry out: *"I'm as old as the forest, but never before have I seen such a sight!"*

To this end, her mother tried to cook stew in eggshells, and then to brew beer in them, as superstition told her. The baby was not shocked. She was not surprised. She did not cry out. She did not react. She just stared at her mother with cold, knowing eyes.

The wearisome infant was treated cruelly. Her mother wanted to make her scream loudly enough to call the faeries back to rescue her. She was sure she could make them take Hobnail away and return with a beautiful, mortal child. So, scream the tiny baby did. But they never came.

In desperation one day, the mother seized Hobnail and thrust her into a roaring fire, blazing in the hearth. She had learnt from others that changelings jump up the chimney and then the human child is returned. A hot coal blinded the child in one eye. It became greyed-out. And still she remained.

Despite attempts to drive her away, and living in constant fear of attack, there was nowhere for Hobnail to go. She never returned to the faeries or sprites or elves. She didn't know where to find them, and although many a time she searched, she always returned, despondent. She grew into a wizened youngster, ageing too quickly, and developed a cunning mind that no one could trust. She appeared to be able to read people's thoughts and was always one step ahead of all around her. She frightened everyone with her dark feelings and scowling face.

Eventually, as years passed, Hobnail was left alone. Her mother died and, although an aged aunt taught her special skills for life, she did not want to share her home with her great-niece.

Warty Toad heaved a mournful groan. "This is tragic!" he declared. "Poor, poor Hobnail! Twelve fingers, broken back, blind eye, no love – oh it is terrible!"

His mistress favoured him with a reassuring smile.

"This is all being passed now, Warty. I has my own home and my friends in you two! My fingers is useful to be having, and my greyed-out eye is helping me always to plot and plan. My bent back worries me not a small jottery; I can walks and rides my wheel-cycle. I lives forever and I lives how I wants." There was a slight hesitation. "But no ones is loving me ever, except you two."

Snidey Slug wrinkled an anxious brow as if he were thinking a lot about what he'd heard. Then his face cleared.

"I don't believe in changelings," he announced. "I think it was just an excuse that people used when their baby was born with problems. I think they were just scared of anything that was unusual. I think they used the changeling idea to be cruel."

Hobnail looked at the little pet gently. "Wise words, indeedy," she nodded.

Warty Toad, as usual, did not want to be left out.

"I don't think you're a changeling!" he declared. "I think you are lovely." He paused. "I think you are just a little… different."

Another smile, perhaps a little wider this time, and a pat on his head, sent a rush of love to his toady heart.

"I *is* different, my Dear Ones," Hobnail agreed. "I *strives* to be different! My aunt, long time ago, is teaching me skills and magical uses for my extra fingers. She is teaching me big lots: most of alls, how to live when others wants me gone. And now I lives and lives." Their mistress yawned and began to snuggle down under the straw sack. Her story was done for the night and she grew sleepy. Her voice was soft. "I sees trees grow tallsome from seedlings, standing for year after year and then I sees them crashing to the ground. I sees all people comes and goes. Comes and goes. Comes and goes." Another yawn. "As time passes."

The two pets knew it was time to rest. They had had a busy day, searching for findings under the long, green, slime fronds and they were happy with their success. Both thought about what they had heard as they drifted off to sleep. They now knew the name of their mistress and why she was blind in one eye. They now knew about her twelve fingers and her hunched back. They now knew she was very, very old and had lived through many years of change, keeping her secret life hidden from others who despised her for being different. They knew a *little* about changelings – and felt somewhat alarmed about faeries, sprites and elves. They wondered about the human babies who were supposed to have been taken to live in the forest: what kind of a life would they have had with the fae creatures? Did they learn how to become faeries themselves? Did they *ever* get rescued? So many questions chased their thoughts, as their eyelids drooped.

There was one thing they did know for certain though. Their mistress loved her Dear Ones. She needed to love, and to be loved, so they were her precious pets. They were all she had. They would stay at her side, loyal and true, all striving to be different, together.

Chapter Three

"So what did she find, Mrs. Mushrump?"

"Hard to say, Mr. Mushrump, hard to say."

"But she went under Great Boulder into the Dark Hole, didn't she, Mrs. Mushrump?"

"Oh yes. She did that, Mr. Mushrump. That she did."

"So what did she put in the Dark Hole, Mrs. Mushrump?"

"I'm not *certain*, Mr. Mushrump. Like I say, it's hard to say, hard to say."

"But can you hazard a guess, Mrs. Mushrump?"

"Oh yes. I can hazard a guess, Mr. Mushrump. I can hazard a guess."

"And, Mrs. Mushrump? And?"

"Like I say, it's hard to say, Mr. Mushrump, hard to say, but it *might* have been…"

"Might have been *what*, Mrs. Mushrump? He'll want to know, you know."

"I know, Mr. Mushrump. I know he'll want to know what I know. Thing is, I'm not sure if I should tell him what I know, you know, in case what I know isn't right."

"They were with her though, weren't they, Mrs. Mushrump?"

"Oh yes, Mr. Mushrump, that they were. Well, at least the toad was, following in her footsteps, plopping along as always. Hard to say where the slug was though. Hard to say, Mr. Mushrump."

"Then, Mrs. Mushrump, they *will* have found some things, won't they?"

"Like I say, Mr. Mushrump, hard to say, but…"

"But *what*, Mrs. Mushrump? What do you think they might have found? What do you think they might have hidden away, this time? We'll have to tell him, Mrs. Mushrump. We'll have to tell him."

"Well, I can't be too sure, Mr. Mushrump, but I *think* she might have had some gold and turquoise butterfly bits."

"Aah. Did she now, Mrs. Mushrump? Did she now?"

"Like I say, Mr. Mushrump, hard to say. Hard to say."

The autumn morning had beaded the hedgerow cobwebs so that their lacy fronds could be seen quite clearly, clinging precariously and swaying gently, with every murmur of the breeze. It was early; so early that the fields around the cottage were still waiting for the morning sunshine to lift their blanket of mist. With the *ting-ting!* of a bicycle bell, a figure disappeared down a little-known path, heavy, muddied boots pushing hard against the pedals, breath steaming in the cold air. The hat on her head was pulled down well so that the black net kept her features hidden, although the hook of her nose still showed, just touching the whiskers on her chin. A pirate patch covered the opaque, grey-blueness of her blind eye. Her hair was pulled back into a tight knot at the nape of her neck, held in place with a shiny, tortoiseshell spike. It was convenient always to have a spike to hand. There were so many things to spike in a day.

It was difficult to cycle over the stones and pebbles which made up the path to the cliffs. They jolted the bicycle, the rider and the two passengers in the basket, who bobbed along feeling rather queasy. It was a good job, then, that Hobnail had travelled this path many times on her way to the sea, otherwise one unexpected rock, one unknown divot, one careless waggle of the handlebars and they would have been flung out of the basket and off the bicycle.

As usual, they passed Badgers' Bank, the claw marks in the earth showing activity of the previous night. The setts were quiet now, amongst the hollows and dips, their occupants no doubt happily snoring away bellies full of earthworms. The windswept field and open pasture lay before them. Noble sheep munched dully on the scrubby grass, their wool parting in the sea breeze. They barely noticed the bicycle and its rider coming to a halt by the cliffs.

"Here we is, my Dear Ones. Out you gets!"

The basket lid was loosened and, with a clumsy tumble of one and a slither of the other, the two pets were at her side. "We's going down to the beach to be charm-stick finding," their mistress continued. "Old charm-sticks is no good at charming, we knows. Path-grits ahead, so pops into my pocket, if you please so."

Warty Toad and Snidey Slug did as they were told. Neither liked the gritty path which clung precariously to the side of the cliff, winding its way down to the shingle beach. In addition, the salty air stung, making cheeks sore and eyes water. However, they both knew that the journey would be worth it, eventually. They could put up with being jostled in the bicycle basket and being cramped in an overcoat pocket, because soon they would be able to enjoy their very favourite games of rock pool fun! Snidey loved the thrill of whoops-a-daisying his way over the seaweed, sliding and slipping, twisting and turning, as Warty laid low pretending to be a stone, waiting for a tasty morsel to crawl over him, unaware of how easily he could cram his mouth. Many a happy hour had been spent like this, as their mistress went beachcombing and muttering her way across the shore.

And so, two black boots wound their way down the tiny, twisting path onto the beach. They stepped carefully between boulders, rocks and stones. They balanced expertly, with only an occasional wobble here and there. They found the rock pools, pausing just long enough to discharge the contents of a certain overcoat pocket, and then they were off again, picking their way through discarded picnic packaging, plastic pots and broken bottles, whose secret messages had long since been blown away by the wind and made unreadable by the tide.

"She is gathering again, Liar-nel."

"So I believe. The Moss-makers told me."

"Mrs. Mushrump can't be sure, but thinks she might have acquired some gold and turquoise butterfly, Liar-nel."

The Leaf Man already knew. He had seen for himself. He smiled a wide smile.

There were bones on the beach. Old, old sheep bones, bleached in the sun and ideal for gathering. Eager fingers grasped a grey skull and plucked it from the shingle. The teeth grinned silently in the jaw; the eye sockets looked vacantly out to sea. It was not at all pretty, but it *was* perfect to position near the Dark Hole, as a warning to the spies to keep away. A little further on, a shoulder blade and some small ribs were collected too. All had been picked clean by the gulls and washed by the seawater. These too, were perfect. They would be ideal charm-sticks; one to wave in the smoky air over her fire, and the others to throw into her copper pot, when needed. They were wrapped in the folds of Hobnail's coat so they would not be dropped, ready to be transported back in the bicycle basket.

For a moment, and smiling with satisfaction, the Collector of Bones straightened her hunched back and scanned the horizon. In the distance, the mouth of her secret sea-cave looked inviting. The tide was just lapping gentle waves at rocks to the entrance. Many a time, she had sheltered inside from a chill wind and a sudden storm. At other times it had been a place where she could sit and think, using her greyed-out eye to muse upon plans and ideas; or it had been a place to light a fire and cook fish; or a retreat when she wished to hide herself away. Now, as always, the cave seemed to call to her, beckoning her to wade out into the water and rest awhile in its cold darkness, but she shook her head. Not today. Things to do. It would still be there, another time.

Shoulders stooped once more, Hobnail made her way along the shore to where she had left her pets. "Charm-sticks is found, Dear Ones. We's just needing crablings for tea and then backs we goes!"

Warty Toad glanced up from his hiding place and looked hopeful. He had developed a taste for many different foods since living with his mistress and was always ready to try a new flavour. It didn't take long for her skilled hands to lift just the right stones and net several baby crabs for the pot. They side-scuttled as best they could to escape, but only succeeded in becoming more entangled and soon, both net and crabs were thrust into an overcoat pocket where they had no choice but to stay still and accept their fate. A few seaweed strands joined them, making them feel a little more at home, for now. Later, they would add just the right amount of brine-flavoured stock to cook with.

Snidey Slug, tired from his play, was relieved to hear they would soon be back in the bicycle basket and on their way. He hoped he would be given an extra-special pat on the head, preferably when Warty Toad was looking, and then he planned to snooze until he was called upon.

The Leaf Man suspected the beachcombers would return to the Dark Hole that evening. He had heard of the collecting, the comings and the goings, the furtive visits back and forth. He could always rely on his spies to keep him informed and it pleased him to know the secrets of the place under the long, green, slime fronds. In good time, he took up position, camouflaged against the trunk of a swamp tree, wrapping himself around it so that he disappeared expertly into the colours and textures of its form. He had his little friends, Fiblet and Fibkin, with him. They hung from Liar-nel's twig-like fingers, cocooned in their leaf beds, eyes closed but ears listening. The Moss-makers knitted away busily, *clack, clack, clack*, at his feet. Mr. and Mrs. Mushrump had taken up their fungus position, near Great Boulder.

Between them, they would not miss a trick.

Ting-ting! The rusty bell cleared the cliff path of noisy seagulls, greedily pecking at the remains of someone's picnic pasty. Up and down the black boots pumped at the pedals and the bent bicycle rattled its way along the stones. Warty and Snidey were bumped around in the basket, along with the

sheep bones, ancient teeth chattering away in the jaws of the skull, giving poor Warty a weird sort of feeling which wasn't altogether comfortable. Sometimes, the things collected by their mistress were not terribly pleasant.

Before long though, the bicycle slowed and the jolts became less frequent. With a whine of brakes, and a wheeze of the rider, they came to a stop. The toad, keen to be free of the basket, poked his head out and looked around him. They were at the edge of the forest and here the bicycle journey had to end. In one flump, he was on the ground, eyes popping, waiting for instructions. The slug followed, slithering his way down the frame until he slipped onto the grass, still wet from the morning's mist.

"Come now, you two!" Hobnail whispered, as she always did. "The time is sun-dialling fast and soon the dimsk will be upon us. We must quick-hurry to beat it."

The two pets knew they should be on their way through the forest trees to the place under the long, green, slime fronds as quickly as possible. They knew they had to be at the Dark Hole before nightfall. Gathering the sheep's skull and charm-stick bones, the figure of their mistress led the way, single eye darting, ever wary. Every now and then her overcoat pocket twitched; the crablings were fighting in their net, tangling and tiring themselves in a futile struggle for freedom. Within minutes, there was a familiar drip,

drop,

    dribble,

        drobble.

They knew that they were nearing Great Boulder.

All made their way in silence, Warty Toad and Snidey Slug following the booted footsteps ahead of them, hopping and plopping, slipping and sliding. They were both excited, and a little bit nervous. Days of collecting, such as these, could mean only one thing – especially if charm-sticks were involved. Tonight would be a night underground. Tonight they would not return to the tumbledown cottage with its welcoming piles of bricks and clinging ivy. Tonight they would prepare themselves for the day ahead.

A rustle of leaves.

    Ears listening. Eyes now open.

    A rippling in the moss and a steady *clack, clack, clack.*

    A nudge and a "shhh!" between two mushrooms.

Great Boulder had rolled from its resting place and not quite closed over the Dark Hole. A wisp of smoke floated through the small gap and wafted gently through the dinge as a familiar chant was heard. Below, twelve fingers opened and closed around a large, copper pot.

"Come sparks and come flame,
Bring yourselves to me!
Underneath this cooking pot
So we can have some tea!"

Soon, smoke began to billow from underneath the pot, followed quickly by blue flames which began to lick between the small black rocks, becoming hotter and turning orange within seconds. An occasional flare created sparks which fire-worked their way upwards to Great Boulder, hissing as they extinguished themselves on its underside bottom. The covering of the Dark Hole steamed and blistered as Great Boulder winced, then grumbled and moaned into the dark forest.

Immediately irritated, Hobnail clambered onto the first few rungs of an old ladder which leant against the wall of her underground chamber, took the tortoiseshell spike from her hair and stretched up. "Great Boulder!" she spat. "Is you fussing and grumble-groaning again? You must always quiet-silent in the forest, being. Liar-nel will us be hearing. Remembers, Great Boulder, spikes be nastier than sparks, you is knowing; spikes be nastier than sparks!" And with that, she spiked Great Boulder's bottom several times with her tortoiseshell barb, as Warty Toad and Snidey Slug closed their eyes and clamped their mouths tight-shut.

"Quiet-silent now, Great Boulder, and no more grumbelations, if you please so!"

With considerable effort, Great Boulder held its breath and did stay silent. It was true that a sudden jab with a spike was far worse than a hot spark and he certainly didn't want any further punishment.

Having descended the ladder back to the floor of the Dark Hole once more, Hobnail swirled a practised hand around, inside the copper pot.

"Cooking pot, cooking pot,
Fill yourself with water
For me to cook myself a feast
Fit for a changeling daughter!"

With a *swoosh!* the pot was full and water whirled in bubbling splashes, heating quickly. Steam curled its way upwards, condensing on Great Boulder's bottom and dripped back into the pot. As the seaweed was tossed in, the two pets watched their mistress lick her hands and rub her lips.

"Crunchy-crablings, if you please so, Warty!"

The toad poked his greedy face into an overcoat pocket and retrieved a fidgeting net. Taking part of it in his mouth, he dragged it, with the unfortunate contents, to the cooking pot. An eager hand grabbed the bundle, made a hole in the side with the fierce jabbing of a finger, and emptied the baby crabs into the seething seaweed water. Within minutes of their arrival, a delicious crab stew was cooked and all were seated around the remains of the fire.

Great Boulder, rather sore from being smoked, sparked and spiked, shuffled slightly to let the last of the steam out of the Dark Hole. It spiralled through the forest, taking the smell of freshly cooked crablings with it.

"Do you think they are feasting, Mrs. Mushrump?"

"Hard to say, Mr. Mushrump, but I would say so, yes."

"Do you think they are getting ready for tomorrow, Mrs. Mushrump?"

"Hard to say, Mr. Mushrump, but I would say so, yes."

"Thought so, Mrs. Mushrump. Thought so."

Once the shells had been cracked open and the sweet crab meat had been picked and pulled out with long finger nails to distribute amongst them, the three settled down. The Dark Hole was becoming darker with every dying flicker of flame, leaving just the glowing embers to warm their faces. As was always the way, Snidey Slug slithered up to perch on Hobnail's shoulder. He liked to nestle against her cheek like this, feeling special and cherished. Warty Toad slowly crept under one smelly armpit, where, as always, he kept warm and a little damp. Their mistress pulled a sack stuffed with collected seagull feathers over her and rested her head against a rock. It wasn't luxury, but they were fed and snug and together, which was all that mattered. For a few moments, they were silent.

Just breathing.

Just thinking.

Just…

…then Snidey shuffled a little.

"Umm… are we going to have a story, tonight?" he asked, hesitantly.

His mistress smiled in the red glow. Her seeing eye was as black as the rocks under the cooking pot. "Not tonight, my Dear One," she replied. "Tonight is for rest-sleeping to prepares us for the morrow."

"So are we going to be busy tomorrow?" came a muffled voice from her armpit.

"We is."

"Are we going to help?"

"You is."

Another smile and a long, slow yawn.

"Quiet hush now, I is needing snore-time, if you please so."

Chapter Four

Gradually, the green dinge lightened with the dawn of the sky above the long, green, slime fronds. Great Boulder shifted slightly to ease its position over the Dark Hole and waited. There would be considerable activity below, today, and it was imperative to remain alert to avoid spikes, and the inevitable sparks, which would be flying upwards. It shuddered slightly at the thought of the barb of the previous night, so the ground trembled and took waking vibrations down to the sleepers below.

A single eye opened. A scowl followed. "Is you being earth-quakery, Great Boulder?"

Silence.

"Because I is not enjoying it. Being a front door to my dark den here, is meaning you is quiet and still-sitting until I is needing you to open or close. Is you ear-attending, Great Boulder?"

Silence.

With a disgruntled snort, Hobnail flung back her seagull feather sack and swung her knobbly feet onto the ground. The dust from last night's fire had settled on the rocky ledges of the walls and cut-out foot holes. These were well-worn now and some were so crumbled that Hobnail had to take care in choosing ones she could rely on, to hold her safely. She took a moment to admire the cobwebs which festooned corners of the Dark Hole, hanging like curtains, draping over shelves which were jam-packed with findings from their collecting expeditions. There were jars and bottles and boxes. There were lotions and potions and powders. There were tonics and slimes and poisons.

There was even a jar of screams…

One wall was particularly special: the Forbidden Wall. Hobnail knew it held all manner of tasty morsels of interest to Warty Toad. This was where she kept red, special-shiny beetles; black, special-shiny beetles; worms, wood lice and spiders; dead dung flies; bird bits – pecky, poky beaks, claws, eyes, tongues, and sad, sad songs – all shut up in containers. There were glow worms in glass bottles, to be shaken awake when extra light was needed, and rotting swamp tree bark, fermenting nicely, to add to a concoction when necessary. This Forbidden Wall was where the collected bones were placed, carefully stacked and tidied away.

It also housed the crushed, gold and turquoise butterfly. Hobnail laced up her boots and inspected them. A small piece of crabling shell was stuck to one toe cap. She removed it, speedily, with well-aimed spit and a quick scratch of a long fingernail. Today, as every day, there was no need to get washed

or dressed as she wore the same grubby, grey tunic, constantly, and a quick swill of her mouth with rainwater was all that was required to clean her grimy teeth. Hobnail's hair though, was a different matter. It was her one excuse for vanity. She used an old, chipped mirror to examine herself, frowning at the cross face which stared back at her. She insisted on wearing her hair tied back in a knot and it had to be a deep shade of damson. Always. Of course, her hair was not naturally of this colour; it had become fog-grey many, many years before she even lived in her tumbledown cottage, but this damson was a colour she favoured and so she dyed her untrimmed lengths frequently. Bottles of cordial were prepared each autumn, from pokeweed berries which hung on the large, red-stemmed plants which she had encouraged to grow along the wild hedgerows of the disused farm track which led to her home. If pokeweed berries were not available, or if all the cordial had been used up, Hobnail expected Warty Toad and Snidey Slug to improvise with the juice of everyday, non-shiny, red and black beetles.

This was the case today.

Upon hearing their mistress smack her hands together in a no-nonsense sort of way, both Dear Ones opened their eyes and blinked.

"Be of waking in nature, you two! I is needing my hair dye and I has things to be doing, you both knows. Chip-choppery, quick-stickery, if you please so."

With that, Hobnail prodded Warty Toad's tummy making him wince and Snidey Slug was tipped out of a jam jar lid where he had slithered to settle down the night before. He fell to the floor of the Dark Hole, landing with an *oomph!* which quite took his breath away and it was a few minutes before he felt recovered. Black and red beetles were located with speed; Warty Toad was particularly good at listening for the familiar scratch-scritch-scratch in parts of the muddy walls or on the dirty floor. Silently, he crept up on the unsuspecting prey and waited. As was often the case, the beetle sensed his presence and lay still for a minute. Warty Toad held his breath... Then, when the beetle thought all was clear, it began to scratch-scritch-scratch again until – *POW!*

Warty Toad smacked it across the back with a well-aimed blow. The dazed beetle was then flicked expertly to Snidey Slug who, realizing he had to get busy and not spend too long wheezing, brought up the rear. When a second unfortunate beetle was flicked Snidey's way, he produced some extra sticky slime to sandwich the two together. This prevented any escape and they could be stored on a stone which had a groove running down the centre. At the end of the groove was a small collecting dish, made of shell.

Hobnail loved this dish. She had found it on the beach one day and polished it until rainbow flashes shone in her face. It was her special hair dye dish. She had few really pretty things. She usually kept items for practical reasons only and there was very little colour in her life. But this dish had been different; it was not only practical, but beautiful as well, and she hadn't been able to resist its girly charm.

"Ahoy down there!" Warty Toad shouted to Snidey in an important fashion. Now that enough beetles, of the right colours, had been stuck together, Warty Toad had made a slow, bobbing ascent to a ledge in the rock just above the stone. "Watch out below Slug-Face!"

With that, he launched himself off the rock to land right on top of the beetles below. *SPLAT!*

Straight away, the fresh beetle juice trickled out from underneath the toad's bulging belly and gradually made its way down the groove in the stone. With a gentle plip-plop, the hair dye dripped into Hobnail's shell dish and collected in a small pool.

"Ha!" cried Warty, thoroughly enjoying himself. He got up from the stone, stood over the groove and scraped the remains of squashed beetle from his belly. He then began his climb once more, to repeat the process. Each time Warty Toad jumped, he gave a yell of excitement which Snidey didn't consider altogether necessary:

"WAHOO!" and –

"YIPES!" and –

"ONE, TWO, THREE, LOOK AT MEEEEeee!"

At the end of the dye-making, Snidey Slug had a ferocious headache and Warty Toad was quite worn out. Between them, they pushed the shell dish over to Hobnail so that she could pour the dark, purple juice through her hair, in syrupy trickles, and they rested whilst she scrunched it and shook off the excess like a dog after a swim.

"What's that peculiar crying noise, Mrs. Mushrump?"

"Hard to say, Mr. Mushrump, hard to say."

"But you did hear it, didn't you, Mrs. Mushrump?"

"Hard to say, Mr. Mushrump, but I think so."

"So what is it, Mrs. Mushrump? What is it?"

"Hard to say, Mr. Mushrump, hard to say, but..."

"But *what* Mrs. Mushrump? *What?*"

"Well, it sounds rather like an animal, Mr. Mushrump."

"An animal, Mrs. Mushrump? An animal? Is that what you think, Mrs. Mushrump? A peculiar noise like that? An animal?"

"Like I say, Mr. Mushrump, hard to say. Maybe? Hard to say."

Hobnail, satisfied with her hair colour, reached up and selected a large battered pan from a rocky area where she kept her cooking pots, utensils, mouse traps and crabling nets. Next, she grabbed a well-used book from a shelf and blew the dust off. "Now my Dear Ones," she announced in a business-like fashion, "firstly is first things! Wood louse jam, if you please so."

Warty Toad slobbered at the thought. "My favourite! Coming, Mistress," he croaked, bubbling spit into his fat throat in anticipation of jam-testing. "Always ready to help!"

"I bet you are!" sneered Snidey Slug turning up his little pug nose in disgust. "*Any* kind of food is your *'favourite'*! It's a wonder you don't burst when you splat those beetles for Mistress's hair dye." He considered Warty's belly from a safe distance. "But then you are like a bouncy ball, so I suppose that helps…" He pursed his snidey lips in pleasure. It was so very satisfying, being horrid, sometimes.

Warty took no notice. He hurried over to Hobnail and assisted until all the ingredients were in the pan. Within minutes, the bubbling mass was steaming Great Boulder's bottom and a delicious smell filled the air. Breakfast was a mouth-watering prospect.

A rippling of moss attracted Liar-nel's attention. A message was passed as the Moss-makers knitted.

Exactly what *was* out there? Crying.

Clack, clack, clack.

Hearing nothing unusual herself, Hobnail licked the end of each of her twelve fingers and smiled at her reflection in the chipped mirror. "I is enjoying my woodlouse jam, Dearies. I is happy-feeling with my hair. I likes being plum colourated."

Her two Dear Ones bobbed up and down in agreement.

"Most peoples is not having hair like this," their mistress continued as she turned this way and that. "I is proud to be different." She paused, for effect. "I is doing it so well so."

Then, without warning, a cloud appeared to cross her face. She closed her good eye to allow her greyed-out one to think. A dark scowl replaced her smile as Hobnail crouched on the stony floor, muttering under her bad breath. Warty Toad and Snidey Slug knew the signs. They took cover, to ride the storm that was undoubtedly brewing.

"But respect and manners is what I wants."

Their mistress drew her feet up and began to rock. And then to shout:

"I SEES YOU, MISS PRISSY!"

Twelve fingernails dug into the palms of her grimy hands as she clenched her knuckles, making them crack.

"I KNOWS where you is living in your clean popsicle dress, with blondiness of hair and whiteness of teeth!"

Hobnail's grey eye watered. Thinking. Planning. She drew a deep breath and spoke in a childish voice:

"Oh no! I can't give you a drink of water! You are a vile-looking old woman. You will dirty my dress. Go away, smelly!"

More rocking. More fist clenching.

"Ands I was *so* thirsty feeling. I was *so* needing of water for my throat to cool. Ands dids Miss Prissy listen? Is she helping of me?"

Warty Toad and Snidey Slug stayed still. They both knew of the incident and they knew exactly who was in trouble. The young girl had shunned Hobnail one day when she had asked for water. She had been rude and unkind. She saw only a disfigured, hunched, old crone, blind in one eye, with begging hands. The begging hands did not touch her heart. They frightened her. She had screamed and shouted, refusing to have anything to do with the stranger.

"I sees into her mind with my third eye," Hobnail continued to mutter. "I is knowing her bad, bad thoughts of me."

The Dear Ones listened sympathetically. It was wrong of the girl to judge someone by the way they looked. All Hobnail wanted was a glass of water. They waited, knowing the outcome of this crouching, rocking and muttering. It was not going to be pretty for Miss Prissy.

Hobnail blinked open her good eye and leapt to her feet. "HOW I HATE HER, IN HER PERFECTION!"

Snidey Slug hissed and sissed in approval and called out: "Do away with her, Mistress! Do away with her!"

Warty Toad swallowed a lump in his bulging throat. This was all a bit scary for him and made him want to hide under a rock. He cowered as Hobnail darted backwards and forwards in a frenzy, flinging ingredients into her copper pot. Jars and tubs and boxes came tumbling down from the Forbidden Wall, their contents snatched and grabbed.

"How DARES she be treating me like that?"

"Do away with her, Mistress! Do away with her!"

Hobnail's hot rage bubbled up inside her like the contents of her pot. She cursed and muttered; she screeched and yelled. Her seeing eye flashed and her body quivered with fury; she seemed to be lost in her incantations as she swirled and whirled around the Dark Hole.

"How dares she so beautiful being and no respecting of me?"

"Do it, Mistress! Do it!"

The copper pot smoked and sparked. A great bubbling noise was heard. It had started. Her voice began low and sinister.

"Little Miss Perfect is you be,
But I is clever and powerful, see,
Gone is your beauty and vanity,
When you wakes up, you is uglier than me!"

Hobnail danced, dizzying herself into a blur, waving the sheep's shoulder around her head. Now she called out, wildly:

"Wash your hands, oh enemy of mine
For you is never getting rid of all your grime!
Is you smoothing your clothes, all ill at ease?
Never is you ironing away the crease!
Ands your hair – you brush ands braids it so
Buts those tangles NEVER will go!"

The Dark Hole was filled with shooting colours from the copper pot. Warty Toad coughed and spluttered; Snidey Slug blinked his stalky eyes as they watered. Their mistress shrieked.

"Ands cry, Miss Prissy! Cry all the while –
Peoples is NEVER seeing your happy smile!"

There was a tremendous *BANG!* The Dark Hole shook. Hobnail fell to the ground in a heap.

Fiblet and Fibkin also heard the peculiar, animal cry.

Liar-nel heard it, too.

It came from the depths of the forest.

"What was that I heard, my little leaf friends?" the Leaf Man asked, quizzically raising an eyebrow, testing them.

"I didn't hear anything!" announced Fiblet, confidently.

"Me neither!" declared Fibkin.

"Well done, my leaflettes," grinned Liar-nel.

Warty Toad and Snidey Slug cleared away the mess quickly, and soon the Dark Hole was in order. Hobnail roused from her sleep and gathered them to her. "I is pleased being with you, my Dear Ones," she purred, stroking their backs with her long fingernails. "Little Miss Prissy Perfect is not so perfectly being now, is she?"

"Nope," replied Warty.

"I still think you should have done away with her!" Snidey whined, disappointed that his role in the whole affair had been limited. "She's only going to be ugly, dirty and have tangles in her hair... and she'll cry a bit."

"I is lesson teaching her. No more is being needful, but I is thanking you for your suggestion making, Snidey," smiled Hobnail indulgently. "Now is cruel man's turn."

It was rare that their mistress should mix with people from the town because she knew she was far from welcome there. Occasionally she would walk cautiously through the streets to find food in bins, if she had not had time to forage for herself, or set mousetraps. If the walk had been long, she sometimes asked to sit for a while or, as was with Miss Prissy, to have a glass of water. Her two Dear Ones often wondered if she did this to test people's reactions to her; to see if their attitude towards her had improved. Inevitably, she would return to her cottage or the Dark Hole, embittered and resentful.

The cruel man in question had shut his shop door in her face. He had not wanted her to dirty his premises and frighten his customers.

"Cruel man with a mind that is as closed being as his door! All I is wanting is respect and manners."

Hobnail's nostrils flared in anger as she worked her plans through her greyed-out eye. Before Warty Toad could find a hiding place, she had begun her low chanting, once more.

"You, man! You who shut the door!
You of hard heart will sell no more!
Your people will always disgusting you find
You, man, with your nasty clos-ed mind!
They will not be buying your thing-a-me-bobs
You'll spend your time crying, as your family sobs.
Just be thinking, as you weep, of me and my face –
And the day you shunned me, away from your place!"

Hobnail threw her arms up into the air, clutching her small charm-stick bones. A short zap of electricity seemed to shoot from her sixth fingers, as the ribs were flung into the pot. There was a tremendous *BANG!* The Dark Hole shook. Hobnail fell to the ground in a heap.

A large black crow flew through the forest. He had some very important information for Liar-nel. *Crauk! Crauk!*

Chapter Five

Both Warty Toad and Snidey Slug needed some fresh air. They knew that their mistress should be left to recover from her toils and the best thing they could do, after tidying up once more, was to make themselves scarce. The long, green, slime fronds dripped,

dropped,

dribbled

and drobbled

onto their backs as they plopped and slithered along.

"All got a bit exciting in there, didn't it?" Warty Toad commented, still shivering at the thought of the noise, sparks and commotion.

"Were you scared?" questioned Snidey, half-smiling.

Warty shrugged his toady shoulders and swallowed. He thought it best not to reply because Snidey Slug was obviously beginning to make fun of him.

"Thought so!" Snidey smirked. "Mistress appreciates my assistance, you know. She wouldn't want *me* to hide under a rock."

Once more, Warty Toad kept quiet. It was always the way with Snidey. He took any chance he could to score points; he always considered himself the Favourite One, even though Warty knew Hobnail treated them both with the same amount of affection. He could be a very annoying slug.

Their plan was to make slow progress in a circle, going around the swamp trees and returning to the Dark Hole in time for something to eat. They carried on for a short while, trying their best to ignore each other when, seemingly from nowhere, a peculiar noise was heard. Their plopping and slithering came to an abrupt halt. They both looked around, eyes bulging and stalks waving with sudden curiosity. The sound came again.

It was a faint cry.

It seemed to be like the pitiful mewing of a lost cat.

It was not a wailing or a howling or a screaming. It was soft and sad, as if the creature was giving up hope.

Warty looked at Snidey. Snidey looked at Warty. Whatever could it be? It was unheard of to find a *new* creature here, under the long, green, slime fronds. The two had traipsed after their mistress so often that they both knew every sound there could possibly be. They knew the way some of the trees creaked; they knew how Great Boulder grumbled; they knew about the rippling of the moss, the mumbling of mushrooms and the crauk of a certain crow – but this was different.

"What is it?" Snidey Slug asked Warty, feeling uneasy.

"No idea," whispered the toad. "Perhaps we ought to venture a little to the right, through those marshy places, to the far trees over there, and find out."

Snidey Slug became a little pale. His soft belly seemed to sink into the path. "I'm not sure we should, Warty. Let's go back and tell Mistress."

Warty Toad looked at his companion, sudden amusement in his eyes. "Is the Favourite One a little, tinsy bit scared, hmm?" he queried. "Do you want to hide under a rock?"

Snidey glowered and his face flushed pink. "No, I certainly do *not*!" he hissed. "I just think we ought to be careful. It might be a trap." And then, to emphasise his point, he added, "The Leaf Man might be playing a trick, you know."

This was true. Both of them knew that Liar-nel was in these parts and that he was keeping an eye on them all. They also knew that he was not to be trusted.

As they paused to consider their options, the creature cried once more. This time, the sound was broken, interrupted by snatches of heartrending sobs. Warty Toad was alarmed now. The only other time he had heard anything similar was when Hobnail had returned to her tumbledown cottage one evening, distraught, because a little boy had been seized quickly from her, by the mother who had accused her of kidnapping. Hobnail had only been trying to help. The child had seemed lost and upset and she had scooped him up in her arms to comfort him, to reassure him. The woman had not seen Hobnail's compassion. The woman had not seen the tenderness in Hobnail's eyes. She saw only what she wanted to see: an old, wizened crone, with a hunched back and deformed hands, holding *her* child. The accusations and shouting-fuss of it all had sent Hobnail fleeing back to her home, confused and distressed. It had taken a while for her to calm herself. She needed many cups of fennel tea, made by Warty, and lots of soothing whistles from Snidey Slug. As she settled, she had made sad, snatching sounds just like this.

Warty Toad could stand it no longer. Something out there needed help.

"There is a strange noise, Liar-nel."

"So I believe. The Moss-makers told me."

"Mrs. Mushrump can't be sure, but she thinks it's a sort of animal, Liar-nel. Crying, Liar-nel. A sort of animal, crying."

The Leaf Man already knew what it was. Crow-cus, the Baby-Snatcher, had reported to him. He smiled a wide smile.

Crauk! Crauk!

Hobnail had slept heavily after her work in the Dark Hole and now she was refreshed. She was very satisfied with the way she had dealt with little Miss Prissy Perfect and the cruel man. She felt she had struck them where it would hurt most, without causing too much damage. She sniffed and turned a proud face up to Great Boulder; she certainly *could* have done more, had she wanted to.

"Respect and manners is all I is wishing for," she muttered again as she rummaged around on a shelf, looking for a little something to eat. It was just as she was chewing on some ginny-spinners, trying to remove their thin legs from between her teeth, that Great Boulder began to grumble and shift slightly, above her. "Great Boulder, is you being grumbelacious for nothings again or is you letting my Dear Ones back into my secrecy place?"

Hobnail's questions were answered almost immediately when Snidey Slug squeezed through a tiny gap and catapulted himself to her feet, in a flurry of flying slime. Another grumble from above allowed the gap to widen slightly and Warty Toad hurled himself down, dropping to the floor, his double chins double-bouncing. Both were obviously in a panic.

"Graciousness, Dear Ones!" their mistress exclaimed. "Whatever is happenings to makes you both so hurry-scurry? It's being like a raining of slugs and toads down here!"

The two struggled to catch their breath. They gasped and gulped and wheezed and whistled, both trying to speak at the same time.

"Be of calm in nature!" Hobnail cried in some dismay. "I is not understanding your speaking and squeak-making. Comes to me and lets me be settling your agitations!"

So saying, the two little pets were scooped up in grimy hands and held close. Warty Toad's thumping heart began to slow, although he blinked his swollen eyes rapidly. Snidey Slug squirmed his way up Hobnail's chin, over her lips, and nestled safely underneath her hooked nose, looking rather like a fat moustache. Finding she couldn't speak with him in that position, Hobnail gently plucked him off her face and slipped him behind one ear, like a pencil.

"Now my frantic pet-lambsicles, what is it you are needing to be telling me? What is it you are in bad states about?"

The two managed to explain, at last.

"By the swamp!"

"On the right of the marshy place!"

"Under a tree!"

"Crying and crying!"

Hobnail's good eye widened as she learnt the reason for their anxiety. Her greyed-out eye was already helping her to think and plan. She heard that Warty had led the way; Snidey had tailed at a distance. They had followed a strange sound, venturing to the right, through the marshy places to the far trees. It had been difficult to see in the gloom of the dinge, but there appeared to be a bundle of bedding tucked in the undergrowth. As they approached, with a great deal of caution, they saw movement.

The bedding was kicking.

The bedding was crying.

The bedding was a baby.

"We're not at all interested, of course," declared Fibkin.

"No! Not one tiny bit," replied Fiblet.

"Do you both think we should keep an eye on her? Do you think we should see what she does?" questioned the Leaf Man.

"No! I think that would be a *very* dull thing to do," smiled Fibkin, turning in his leaf to wink at his brother.

"Very dull. Very boring. No fun at all. It would be the last thing *any* of us would want to do," Fiblet winked back.

"Quite so, my leaflettes," the Leaf Man nodded.

Hobnail gathered an old blanket around her shoulders and pulled on her boots. There was no time to lose. If Crow-cus found him, the baby would be in the Leaf Man's hands. They had all heard the *crauk!* of the crow in recent days, and they suspected he was up to no good. They were also aware, that the Leaf Man had his messengers. The news would travel fast.

"Quick-hurry, Dear Ones," Hobnail urged, beginning to climb the cut-out foot holes in the wall. "We must hasten fastly to retrieve the child. Liar-nel will be on our heels in no minutes!"

Warty Toad and Snidey Slug did not hesitate. It was not their position to question their mistress. If she told them to do something, they jumped to it, and so without pausing to consider how this plan would work out, they followed her speedily out of the Dark Hole. With luck and the cover of dimsk, they would not be spotted. All picked their way carefully through the moss, between stones and rocks, in and out of the trees. They avoided any clutch of mushrooms they saw and kept an eye out for circling birds. They moved silently and swiftly towards the marshy places, hoping and hoping they were unseen.

Liar-nel grinned knowingly as the moss sponged over his feet. Fiblet and Fibkin bided their time, swinging from his twig fingers, in their snug, leafy cocoons. His little plan was working beautifully.

Hobnail's heart melted. The moment she saw the tiny, tearful bundle, she felt a warm rush envelop her. The baby stopped crying immediately and opened his eyes wide. Hobnail put one grimy finger to her lips and, checking right and left, picked the child up. She dangled him in front of her. The little one stared at her, in complete trust and innocence.

"Be hushed now little, wet baby-face," Hobnail soothed. "You is coming with us to be safe kept and happy made."

The baby continued to gaze at her, teardrops collecting on his eyelashes like morning dew in a spider's web.

"I is thinking you is gift-being for me and I is warm-feeling about you, my lovely," Hobnail murmured. "Shhh now. Be tranquil in baby-mind."

So saying, she straightened her back as best she could and, hiding the baby under the folds of her blanket, she began to make her way through the trees. She quivered with excitement, hardly believing her luck, for Hobnail had long since given up hope of ever having a child of her own. She had learnt to be content with her life under the long, green, slime fronds, accepting that she would live alone, apart from odd, little animal friends, but had often wondered what it must be like. And now this! A baby sweetheart here in the forest. All hers! A chance to love – and be loved – at long last.

Snidey Slug and Warty Toad listened to their mistress and felt a little concerned as they followed, slithering and sliding, plopping and squelching through the mud and slime. Hobnail closed her good eye to allow her greyed-out one to think as she crept along, keeping her ears alert and her nose sharp. She did not need to see where she was going; she was very familiar with all routes through the place under the long, green, slime fronds and with other senses heightened, she knew she would be warned in good time of any danger.

It would be foolish to take the baby back to the Dark Hole. There was too great a chance of Liar-nel finding out and if he decided to camp by Great Boulder, there would be no escape. The best thing to do would be to take the trembling poppet back to her cottage. Once there, Hobnail could consider what her options were. Firstly, there would be practical issues to deal with: food, drink, clothing and where the poor, little thing would sleep. Oh – and nappies. Secondly, there were other matters to consider, which were much more difficult. Where did the baby come from? Who did he belong to? Why was he in the forest, hidden under the long, green slime fronds? Could she keep him? *Should* she keep him? And then, what about growing up? A baby was one thing; a great, gangling teenager in her tumbledown cottage, was quite another. Hobnail frowned at the thought. She had come across too many like that in the town and her experiences had not been good.

Warty Toad and Snidey Slug saw their mistress shake her head and heard her chunner under her breath. They knew she was trying to work things out.

This was not going to be easy. Not easy at all.

"I told Liar-nel, Mrs. Mushrump."

"Did you now, Mr. Mushrump? Did you, now?"

"And what d'you think he said, Mrs. Mushrump?"

"That's hard to say, Mr. Mushrump. That's hard to say."

"He said he *knew*. Moss-makers told him, so he knew."

"Did they now, Mr. Mushrump? Did they, now?"

"And do you think Crow-cus is involved, Mrs. Mushrump?"

"Hard to say, Mr. Mushrump. Like I say, hard to say."

Dusk was closing in as the little troupe reached the cottage. The baby had been put into the bicycle basket, still waiting at the edge of the forest, and was unseen. Instructing Warty Toad and Snidey Slug to rekindle the fire, Hobnail made her way to the cellar door. As usual, it was bolted tight shut against unwelcome intruders. This was where she intended to keep the little boy until she thought of a better plan. The bolt took some tugging before it gave way and the door opened with a weary creak. Hobnail stepped carefully into the darkness. In one arm she held her precious discovery, tightly. She certainly did not want to trip and drop him. At the bottom of the steps, she paused, fumbling to locate a large candle and a box of matches. It was not easy to light, single-handed, and the baby, having slept off some of his exhaustion, stirred and whimpered. Hobnail felt the familiar rush of warmth and held him close.

"Be nots afraid, little kipper," she whispered, her whiskery chin close to his soft cheek. "I is mindful in my caringness of you."

The baby locked his eyes on the old, cragged face and slowly placed his tiny thumb into his tiny mouth. He sucked and sucked.

"My little kipper's empty of tummy, I is thinking. Feedings time is upon us already!" Hobnail realised, with a degree of concern. She had not yet worked out the answer to this difficulty. Her meals of squirrel or mouse stew, boiled crablings and woodlouse jam were not suitable, she knew. Nor would it be right to feed the little one ginny spinners or beetles. She knew enough about babies to understand they needed milk, but Hobnail sighed sadly – her own grey teats were withered, shrivelled and useless. She could no more feed a baby than permanently straighten her hunched back.

"I must be answer finding and hard thinking, little kipper."

There in the damp of the cellar, the flickering candle casting long shadows onto the walls, one eye closed and a greyed-out one began to work. She could steal milk, perhaps? There were dairy farmers nearby. Perhaps she could creep into the sheds at night and milk a cow?

No. No. She had tried that in the past and her breath had turned the milk sour, in seconds.

What about swamp tree bark? Could she boil it and squeeze it and make it less bitter with hedgerow blackberries?

No. No. There *had* to be a better way. Somewhere in the past there was a clue. Memories floated in the stillness of the air. Foods of the forest: berries, roots, dandelion leaves, sorrel, nuts...

Nuts!

Hobnail's good eye flashed open and all around her glowed yellow. That was it! She remembered as a child, making her own nut milk when she herself was starving. She gathered the baby to her once more and took the cellar steps in long, loping strides, calling to her Dear Ones urgently. "Warty! Snidey! Hazelnuts if you please so! Find, find, quick-stickery! Be looking in my food storage places, my Dears. Nut milk is being needed, fastly!"

Electric fingers speeded the process of soaking, crushing, straining and squeezing and, within minutes, pure, sweet hazelnut milk was dribbling down the baby's chin, as Hobnail rocked and hummed. Warty Toad looked on in envy. It was a while since he had eaten and it didn't look as if his next meal was happening soon.

The baby guzzled and gulped, greedily.

Night fell over the fields. Night fell over the hedgerows and the twisting lane which led to a tumbledown cottage. Night fell in the forest.

Two small, leafy cocoons opened. One eye winked at the other. With a nod from Liar-nel, Fiblet and Fibkin slipped out of their pouches and dropped from twiggy fingers, to the floor. Whispering excitedly, they tiptoed off.

Chapter Six

Little Kipper was settled at last. The hazelnut milk had been warm and satisfying, and there had even been enough for the others to enjoy. Now, wrapped in an old shawl, tucked up in a musty apple box in the cellar, sweet dreams were floating through the baby's mind as he sucked on his little thumb. Hobnail placed a whiskery kiss on his perfect cheek and made her way up the steps, back to her Dear Ones.

"Kipperling is fastly sleeping in sweet apple loveliness," she announced, with a weary sigh. "Methinks we is needing of a restful bedtime story, my Dears," and lowering herself onto a mouldy sofa she had found dumped by the roadside one day, she added, "You is knowing something of my changeling past, but I must be telling you of my aged aunt." Hobnail paused to remember. "All wise words, she be. All-knowing, clever grower of plants." She chuckled to herself as Warty Toad and Snidey Slug found their special places to snuggle up. "'Know your poisons!' says she. Over and over is she telling me these words: 'Know your poisons! Know your poisons!' And I listens... and I learns... Good listenings always makes good learnings we knows."

Snidey cast his mind back to the last story they had heard. He was keen to show he had been listening carefully.

"Is this the aunt who didn't want to share her home, when you were left alone?" he asked. "Your great aunt?"

Hobnail nodded slowly and spoke softly. "Great Aunt Tabitha Wrinklewarts. Ah, Great Aunt Tabitha."

Warty Toad drew himself up with pride. He felt he had a certain amount in common with this wise, all-knowing, clever aunt. Nonchalantly, he stroked a scabby lump on his forehead and took extra interest in the tale.

Tabitha truly was a sight to behold. She was an ogre of a woman, with enormous, flapping hands and a shock of fiery, red hair which fell in frizzy tumbles around the hanging jowls of her cheeks. Her smile through chipped, stained teeth, was warmly meant, but somewhat alarming; it was a lopsided sort of grimace. Hairs sprouted from her large-lobed, crusty ears, and warts nestled cosily in the furrows of her wrinkles. There was a peculiar smell of sour vinegar about her.

On first meeting Hobnail, she peered down at her disfigured niece, took a deep breath in through the flaring nostrils of her grotesque nose, and roared with laughter. The force of her breath hit Hobnail full-face, like a sudden autumn gale, leaving her lost for words. Hobnail's eyes widened as she lowered her head and gulped.

"SO!" Great Aunt Tabitha Wrinklewarts bellowed. "HERE YOU ARE, ON MY DOORSTEP, AT LAST! WHAT TOOK YOU SO LONG TO SEE YOUR BELOVED OLD AUNTIE?"

Hobnail was lost for words. Her gaze was transfixed on her great aunt's feet. They were barely clad, in massive flip-flops, and they had to be the biggest feet she had ever seen. Corns, callouses and bunions bumped all over them, volcanic and angry. Toes like stone slabs protruded at the front, their nails ridged and yellow with rot.

"WELL?" Tabitha Wrinklewarts boomed, with a piercing stare. "AND ARE YOU IMPRESSED?"

Hobnail attempted to reply, but could only stammer and stutter. She felt hot with embarrassment. What should she say?

"My, my," Tabitha commented, more gently. "Shy are we? Black cat got your tongue, eh?" and she stamped her great feet on the ground in a strange sort of dance, pointing at the huge appendages with pride. "Big, aren't they?" she questioned, not really expecting an answer. "All the better for *lolloping* along, you know. People find it quite frightening if you *lollop* – you really should try it when you're older. You'd do it well with your hunched shoulders!" Then, taking one of Hobnail's hands in her own giant one, she turned and pulled her startled niece into the house.

Warty Toad shuddered a little underneath Hobnail's armpit. This aunt was not someone to meet on a dark night. In fact, he thought, she wasn't someone he would like to meet at all.

In Tabitha's home there was a hearth, and by the hearth was a basket. The lid seemed to lift slightly now and then, and a strange scratching noise could be heard, coming from inside. Tabitha threw some garden cuttings onto her smouldering fire and blew as gently as she could, from underneath. Grey, choking billowings of smoke filled the air, stinging eyes and catching breath. She wafted her hands to encourage flames, and within minutes, the fire had woken up and was burning well. Then she gave Hobnail a wink, picked up the basket and swung it around and around her head, making the smoke swirl in dizzying flurries through the room. Hobnail's eyes watered as she coughed, spluttering and uncomfortable, but before she knew it, the lid was opened and, to her astonishment, four tiny turtles were plucked from within. They dangled daintily from her aunt's rough-skinned hands, squealing and dazed. In no time at all, they were cooking on the fire, shells steaming nicely.

"Turtle sandwich?"

"I, er – is nevers, um, eating of, er – "

"Turtle sandwich?"

"No, nevers! I means yes! They is mouth-watery-making, I's sure."

Thick, grey hunks of grimy bread were cut and each turtle was crammed in between the slices, legs and arms sticking out. Smelling delicious, they were arranged in a pile on a heavy wooden board.

"Do tuck in!" Tabitha urged, helping herself to a particularly large one. "No need for manners!" and she grinned with her mouth stuffed full, a turtle tail showing between her teeth.

Hobnail sighed, pausing in her story. It was the best meal she had ever eaten. Simply scrummy!

Snidey Slug was rather pleased to hear of the turtles' demise. This just showed having a shell was no particular protection. He would stop wishing he had one now. His snail cousins were nothing special after all. Ha.

With the last toenail of turtle swallowed and the crunching of shells finished, Great Aunt Tabitha Wrinklewarts jumped to her feet and clapped her hands together. "We must get on!" she announced. "Come with me, my Peculiar One! I am going to show you a thing or two about potions and poisons. You must pay attention because this is your one and only chance to learn, you know. Nobody in the whole world knows as much about them as I do!" So saying, Hobnail was hauled to her feet. "*Six* fingers?" queried Tabitha, looking at the small hand in her own bear's paw. "Jolly useful. Extra-jolly useful, in fact. Lucky you!"

Her niece smiled happily. As they made their way down an overgrown path, she was beginning to feel special for the first time in her sorry life. This visit was turning out to be better than she had hoped and she was looking forward to learning all she could.

Warty Toad and Snidey Slug were gripped. Little by little they were learning more about their mistress with each story that was told. But, as they listened, they had no idea that two sinister, twiggy creatures were sneaking and snunkling through the moss and dinge, towards the edge of the forest, past the long, green slime fronds which

   dripped,

      and dropped,

         and dribbled

            and drobbled...

The two leaflettes, Fiblet and Fibkin, knew their way well.

In those long ago days, Tabitha Wrinklewarts had a certain reputation. She had special skills in cultivating plants of all types, shapes, colours and sizes, and she delighted in making weird and wonderful concoctions from her unusual herb garden. Admiring the golds, emeralds and violets, the crimsons, azures and corals, occasionally, some people were brave enough to request a plant cutting for their own garden. It took considerable courage to ask – the chance of being given something altogether different was *very* likely – and generally people stayed away. This Titan of a woman was not one to be disturbed as she went about her digging, planting and pruning. She did not especially welcome visitors.

Today, however, was different. Here was a *special* visitor. A special guest with similar interests and abilities, to shape in her own fashion. This was going to be a real treat.

"Your eye," Tabitha commented, as they walked, hand-in-hand.

"Hot coal," replied Hobnail, matter of factly. "When I was thrown into the fire to send me up the chimney, you know."

"No, no, no, no, no! I don't mean *that* one!" her aunt shook her great head and stopped mid-stride. She peered at Hobnail, her own eyes black and shrewd. "Your *inner* eye. Your mind-reading eye. Your future-looking eye."

"My what?"

"Your *inner* eye! Oh yes, young lady. It is there, inside your forehead. Use it well. Read minds, tell the future and be aware of what is about to happen. Protect yourself with it."

Hobnail was puzzled. This was the first time she had heard about her mind-reading eye, but before she could ask about it or consider it further, her attention was drawn to the garden in front of them. She stood, open-mouthed. It was a mass of blooms and a riot of colour. The season was autumn and these plants surely should have been drooping, withered and turning brown. They should have been sorrowfully looking back on their summer days, flower heads bowed and petals tumbled. They should have been limp, sagging and crestfallen; but this was Tabitha Wrinklewarts' garden and there was a certain magic in the air. As a result, the plot was ablaze with reds, oranges, purples and blues. Pinks, apricots, lilacs and turquoises jostled with leaves of sea green, mint and lime, teal, myrtle and olive. There were soft tissue blossoms, just falling open, and thistle spikes and rose thorns protecting their flower crowns. There were stingers and sweet-scenters. There were herbs and hips and haws. Every imaginable plant was thriving and flourishing. Hobnail stared and stared. She was completely dumbstruck.

A slight breeze blew, indicating a coolness in the air all of a sudden. Plucking a few leaves from a nearby shrub, Tabitha turned abruptly, to face her niece. She was unexpectedly severe and frowning. The sun disappeared behind a cloud. "Know your poisons, sweet child! Know your poisons!" She thrust the leaves at Hobnail who shrank back, instinctively. Her great aunt towered over her.

"*Toxicodendron radicans*, my princess: Poison Ivy."

Tabitha pressed her niece's face against the green foliage. She was scowling as she lowered her voice and whispered hoarsely, "Look and learn, Peculiar One. Learn its smell and its feel. Be able to recognise it in the dark, for it will become one of your most loyal and trusted friends – and you have precious few of them! Know your poisons, Little Lady. Know your poisons!"

Releasing her hold on Hobnail, Tabitha Wrinklewarts' face brightened once more. "Very useful basis for all you have to do. Stick a bit of Poison Ivy in your pot and you can't go far wrong!" She grinned and, beckoning her charge with one long finger, lolloped off into the swaying grasses. The sun came out from behind the cloud and the air warmed.

Warty Toad and Snidey Slug waited. Their mistress had stopped telling her story. There was an ominous silence.

"Mistress?"

"Shhhh."

"But –"

"I has but small times left for story-speaking, my Dear Ones. I wills be of continuing in nature, but I might be needing to stop quick-stickery."

Her inner eye had woken up.

A green, leafy stalk with drooping, purple flowers seemed to nod, gently. Happy that her great aunt was in a better mood once more, Hobnail tugged at it and presented her find to Tabitha.

"Pretty, eh?" her aunt questioned, with one eyebrow raised in her wrinkled, warty face.

Hobnail nodded eagerly.

"Pah! Pretty *deadly*, more likely!"

Tabitha Wrinklewarts took the stems from her and kissed the flowers softly, with hairy lips.

"*Belladonna*. My beauteous *Belladonna*! Many have fallen because of her. Some call this plant: 'Deadly Nightshade', you know. It doesn't matter, but I always think *Belladonna* is a much more magical, ladylike name, don't you?"

Hobnail made no reply. Her hands were beginning to itch so she started to scratch them hard with her nails. Her aunt didn't seem to notice.

"Make a cordial with the black fruit of *Belladonna* and you have a very powerful – " She stopped abruptly to consider her niece. "Whatever's the matter?"

"I – I – I is itch-scratching," Hobnail stammered, her face reddening with angry hives. "I – is feeling stranger than I normals do." Her twelve fingers were beginning to swell.

"Ah! I forget you are but a novice in all these things, Peculiar One. Even handling my lovely *Belladonna* can cause suffering, if you are not experienced. You must wash yourself in the barrel of rainwater behind the house; we are going there, directly!"

So saying, hand in hand, they lolloped towards the house, Hobnail repeating and reciting: "Know your poisons! Know your poisons!"

And: "Poison Ivy: a true and trusted friend. Deadly Nightshade: for the bitter end."

And: "Know your poisons! Know your poisons!"

And: "Wash hands! Handle with care! Only use poisons, if you dare!" until her face was washed and her sore hands were scrubbed clean.

Tabitha Wrinklewarts continued to show her understudy mistletoe, wormwood and mandrake, be-still, bloodroot and bluebell. She learnt about monkshood or wolfs-bane, and poppy.

"Wrap seeds of wolfs-bane in lizard skin and carry it with you to become invisible at will. Frightfully good fun! You must try it," Tabitha laughed, promptly disappearing from sight.

She learnt how to choose plants for different purposes; how to set seed and harvest, by the moon. She was told how to keep a garden suspended in mid-summer to ensure the plants were fully energetic and charged. She recited how to deal with rowan, mugwort, sage, and recognised the scents of patchouli, lavender and catnip.

"If you want to make friends with a cat," she was told, "sew love sachets with rose petals and catnip. Your feline acquaintance will never leave your side!"

Hobnail smiled at this. She was very fond of cats. Especially those wicked ones who knew their own minds.

As the end of the afternoon approached, she saw a final plant, not mentioned before. It was tucked away in a corner by the wall and had large, cauliflower heads of tiny white flowers. Eager to show her knowledge at last, Hobnail picked some. "Cow parsley!" she exclaimed confidently, stooping to gather handfuls. "Cow parsley pie is good tastery foodness. I is thinking to make some for us. Would that please-face you?"

Stuffing her pockets full, Hobnail turned to face her great aunt, flower juice dripping off her twelve fingers.

"You call that 'cow parsley'?" Tabitha queried, looking at the plant. "You are mistaken, my Strange Sweetheart!"

"Is right so!" Hobnail insisted. "I is seeing it all overs the fields and I is knowing it is cow parsley. Is right so!"

"Is *wrong* so!" The flowers were dashed from her hands to the ground. "Empty your pockets, child!"

Hobnail did as she was told, without further argument. She felt foolish and frightened. She raised her fingers to her mouth to lick the juice from them…

Warty Toad could stand this story no longer. He dropped from his cosy, armpit bed onto Hobnail's lap, his eyes popping with concern.

"You didn't, did you?" he yelped. "You didn't *lick* your fingers, did you?"

His mistress smiled and patted him, fondly. "I dids not, my dear. I woulds not be here story-telling if I licks my fingers then. I's being deadsies if so's."

Snidey Slug looked at his gulping, panicking friend with disdain. "Stupid," he smirked.

"NEVER lick your fingers in a garden," warned Tabitha Wrinklewarts. "Know your poisons! That, my Foolish One, is *hemlock*. Don't be tricked by its prettiness. Cow parsley indeed!"

With that, the visit was over. Great Aunt Tabitha Wrinklewarts seemed to tire of her guest and told her it was time to leave. "I don't want to see much more of you, Little Lady," she announced. "I expect you to think over what you have learnt today and remember my lessons. I expect you to use your twelve fingers wisely; you will come to appreciate their powers in time."

She thrust a book into her niece's hands as she was shown the way out. It was entitled:

'Magickal Mischief ~

A guide to the secrets of your garden.'

Hobnail was thrilled and looked up to thank her aunt, but she had vanished inside the house with an airy wave of one great hand. All alone once more, the changeling remembered those important words…

"Know your poisons! Know your poisons!" chanted Warty Toad and Snidey Slug in unison, eager to show they had listened.

Hobnail suddenly sat up straight. "NO!" she cried tipping her two Dear Ones to the floor. *'Read minds, tell the future and be aware of what is about to happen!'* I has inner eye workings!"

In a trice she was throwing herself down the cellar steps, crying out, "I is taking Little Kipper to safe-keeping place! I knows who is comings to this door. Be mindful to stop them followings us for I needs time to be hiding my poppet!"

And then she was gone.

Chapter Seven

"I think mischief is afoot, Mr. Mushrump."

"Do you now, Mrs. Mushrump? Why do you think that?"

"Just a feeling, Mr. Mushrump. Just a feeling."

"But what sort of a feeling, Mrs. Mushrump? You can't just say you have a *feeling*. You can have different kinds of feelings, you know. Feelings come in all sorts of colours, Mrs. Mushrump, so what *sort* of a feeling?"

"Hard to say, Mr. Mushrump. Hard to say."

"But you mention mischief, Mrs. Mushrump."

"That I did, Mr. Mushrump. That I did."

"So what makes you think that?"

"Like I say, Mr. Mushrump, it's hard to say."

"Hard to say *what* exactly, Mrs. Mushrump?"

"Hard to say what sort of colour this feeling is, Mr. Mushrump."

"Yellow? Green? Pink? Fluffy cloud colour?"

"No, Mr. Mushrump. This feeling isn't a pretty colour."

"Black? Grey? Brown? Old, mouldy potato colour?"

"Hard to say, Mr. Mushrump. Like I say, it's hard to say."

Warty Toad looked at Snidey Slug.

Snidey Slug shrugged and looked back at Warty Toad.

"Where did she go?" Warty questioned. "Where did she take Baby-suck-Thumb?"

Snidey made no reply but slithered silently to the half-broken door of the ramshackle cottage and peered out, warily. Left. Right. And left again.

"You aren't crossing a road, you know," Warty Toad called out. "Come back in. I was talking to you."

"Well, her bike's gone," Snidey commented, returning, his wet skin cooled from the chill night air. "She must have popped her poppet, into her basket. Poppety-pop."

The two listened as rain began to fall. It was now both dark and wet. They felt quite abandoned and not altogether at ease. Why had Hobnail been in such a scramble to run out into the night? What did she mean about her inner eye working? Was this her third eye then, seeing into the future?

Warty Toad gulped. And exactly *who* did she think was coming to the door? "I think, perhaps, we ought to hide," he whispered. "I think, perhaps, we need to be careful."

It was lucky for Hobnail that the tide was out. Her sea-cave was dappled in shifting peeps of moonlight through the rain, as the night clouds jostled over her head. She breathed a sigh of relief as the sanctuary beckoned her with a mother's arms. Tiny ripplings of water trilled over the sand in gentle rushes, lapping at rocks, making it easy to slosh through. Clutching her precious bundle against her chest like a child with a hot water bottle, Hobnail checked there was no sign of being followed, then slipped inside.

Fiblet and Fibkin knew they would have no trouble entering the dilapidated cottage. They squeezed through the gap in the half-broken door with ease and stood, twiggy legs slightly apart, rain dripping off them.

"Nobody at home?"

"Very surprising."

"Perhaps they *are* at home but don't want to speak to us."

"Even *more* surprising."

"Do you think they are having a game of Hide-and-Seek?"

"Oh goody, goody. I like to seek."

In a swift movement, Fibkin propelled himself upwards, twirling twiggily, to land on top of the old sofa.

"Smells like they've been here recently," he commented.

"All sluggy and toady?"

"Yip."

Fiblet made a pretence of yawning. "You know, actually I'm a little tired to play Hide-and-Seek, Fibkin. I could shout, 'Come out, come out, wherever you are!' but I really can't be bothered. And we've got plenty of time – they've got to come out sooner or later."

Fibkin picked at a little piece of bark, like a scab, on his knee, and flicked it onto the cracked floor slates below him. He grinned at his brother and then, assuming a nonchalant tone spoke out, quite loudly, so that anyone who *might just be hiding* could hear, quite clearly. "It *seems* that your hideously ugly mistress has been misbehaving! It *seems* that the ghastly, awful hunchback is in a *lot* of trouble. We know – and more importantly, the *Leaf Man* knows – that old Missus Twelve-Fingers has got hold of a baby!"

Not a sound was to be heard.

Another skitter of bark was flicked onto the floor.

"Now I *know* I might just be addressing thin (and smelly) air here, but I think you are playing games with us and actually, you can hear every word I drop, like leaf litter, into your dirty ear'oles."

The leaflettes nodded a signal to each other. With an impish glint in his eye, and stealth in his movements, Fiblet began to search. He peeped and poked and pried in every corner, every nook and every cranny. Silently.

Fibkin continued to speak, as if addressing nobody in particular. "The Moss-makers told Liar-nel about a strange sound in the forest. They report back to him, you know. They ripple and burble and pass their messages squashily, from wet lips to wet lips. They are his spies on the forest floor. Their frog-eyes pop up occasionally, as they fiddle and twiddle and knit and crochet the moss, so they always notice things. *Clack. Clack. Clack.* They always notice sights and sounds and smells…"

A pause.

"Your baby was lucky, you know. Your ickle-wickle baby could have sunk in a nasty, mossy marsh."

Another pause, as Fiblet crept around the cottage on soundless, sneaky feet.

"The Moss-makers eat creatures, you know. If you make a mistake under the long, green slime fronds, you can easily end up slipping into their depths. Carnivorous, see, Moss-makers are."

Fiblet tiptoed over the cold floor. He sucked the air in deeply, through tiny holes in his bark. Sniffing them out. He knew the Dear Ones were hiding. He knew he would find them. It was just a matter of time.

"Then, there are the Mushrumps."

Fiblet could detect the sweet, breathy scent of hazelnut milk. He smiled in the darkness as he listened to his twig-twin.

"The Mushrumps are very close to Liar-nel. They move when you can't see them and set up residence at the base of trees, looking for all the world like a pair of fat fungi. They amuse the Leaf Man. He usually knows their news already, but it is useful to corroborate what others have been telling him.

Goodness, they are gossips! They are busybodies! News travels fast from gossips and busybodies."

Fiblet had located them. He stiffened, camouflaged himself and waited, smiling.

"And then there's always Crow-cus."

Another pause.

"And us."

Fibkin was quiet for a moment. He knew his twin-twiglet was poised. He knew Fiblet had found them. He savoured the power of the moment, before whispering into the darkness: "So there's no use denying it. We know what your mistress has done!"

All that could be heard was the rain tap-tap-tapping on the slates. All was absolutely still. The air itself seemed poised. Expectant.

A deep breath – and a sudden *shout!*

"SHE'S STOLEN SOMEBODY'S BABY!"

At the unexpected noise, Warty Toad and Snidey Slug both *shrieked* and tumbled from their hiding places, in a flurry and a kerfuffle, right at the feet of Fiblet. Poor Snidey was a dreadful shade of puce, caused by not daring to breathe enough, and Warty looked decidedly sickly green with fright. His eyes popped and bulged, and he kept gulping and swallowing, quite unable to say a word.

Fibkin joined Fiblet on the floor. They both took deliberate steps towards the Dear Ones and stared at them, menacingly. This was most satisfactory. The Leaf Man would be pleased. They would deliver their mischief-making message in full, now, and scoot home, without difficulty. Excellent!

It was hard to leave. Hobnail lifted her head and gazed out of the mouth of the sea-cave at the rising waters. She knew she could not wait much longer; tide and dawn were against her. She had cosied up Little Kipper in an old shawl, hurriedly grabbed when leaving the cottage, and the tiny child was sleeping soundly. His bed was a secure ledge of rock, safe above the water and he had been swaddled tightly to prevent any wriggling. With care, Hobnail had dangled seashells from seaweed ribbons above his head, so that when he awoke they would catch his eye and amuse him until she could return. For a moment or two, Hobnail allowed herself a daydream.

Wouldn't it be perfect if she could keep him? All hers? Wouldn't it be exciting? And fun! She could teach him all she knew about the wild hedgerows, seashore and forest. She could teach him how to forage and cook. They could gather special ingredients together, under the long, green, slime fronds. She could even teach him copper pot lessons, under Great Boulder, in the Dark Hole! Hobnail smiled wickedly. Perhaps she could pass on her powers... She took a quick peep at the tiny hand which clutched the shawl. Shame he didn't have six fingers, but no matter.

Hobnail shook her head to clear it; she really had to leave now. She must hurry back to her Dear Ones and they must work out a plan, together. She could return in a few hours and bring hazelnut milk. All would be well.

The unwelcome visitors had left the cottage. Warty Toad and Snidey Slug huddled together for comfort. Tonight was no night for petty squabbles and they were glad of each other's company. They quietly thought over what they had heard. There were certain facts which could not be disputed:

1. There was a baby.

2. Hobnail had the baby.

3. The Leaf Man knew she had the baby.

4. The Leaf Man's messengers had been quite clear: they would make sure the people in the town knew about the strange, old crone having a child in her home.

5. Hobnail was in trouble.

Unfortunately, there was only one solution: Little Kipper had to go back. He would have to return to wherever he came from.

Both Warty Toad and Snidey Slug knew that Hobnail had not stolen the baby; indeed *they* had been the ones to find him, but once the wicked word of 'kidnap' spread, there would be no way the truth would come out. How could they, a slug and a toad, explain to anyone what had really happened? And nobody would believe the word of Hobnail – she was reviled enough as it was. No matter how much she begged, or explained, or argued her case, she would be accused of snatching a baby. She couldn't even pretend he was hers; that was obviously quite impossible.

Of course, Fiblet and Fibkin could be bluffing. They could be just making trouble for the sake of it and having a good laugh now, at their expense. They might all be there, in their forest home: the Leaf Man, the leaflettes, the Mushrumps and Moss-makers, all laughing away at their little joke, their little trick, their little scheme. They might have no intention of telling *anyone* about Baby-suck-Thumb, and Hobnail might be quite safe.

But could they risk it?

Warty worried about how to tell their mistress the news. Snidey worried about how they would cope if Hobnail, as Fibkin had promised, was thrown into jail. They both worried about the baby. After all, where *did* he come from? Who *did* he belong to?

Their agitations were brought to an abrupt halt by the sound of the cottage door, opening and closing with its familiar creak.

"My Dears, I is home being," called the well-loved voice. "Has you both been kettle boiling and cups of tea thinking of?"

Hobnail's pets raced to her and both began to jabber at once. It was as if a stretched balloon had been pierced, all the air whistling out garbled explanations which flew in a tangle of confusion around the room. They were desperate to tell her of the twig-twins' visit and their demands. If Fibkin and Fiblet carried out their threat, the whole town would be looking for her soon. All it would take, would be a whisper in someone's ear, an idea in their head, and the secret would be out! The two fibbers could do this, easily.

"Graciousness, Dear Ones! Stop being squeakerish and be settling of calm manner, if you please so! I is never ear listening to noise-makers, so gets my tea and we will be of quiet talking."

Liar-nel nodded as he lay back against the swamp tree branch. Just so. The leaflettes had done well.

Hobnail's greyed-out eye watered when she was told. Planning. Thinking. With sadness. She knew it had all been too good to be true. She would never be able to have a child of her own and her Little Kipper could never be kept a secret. There were too many spies. Her thoughts of caring for the baby with hazelnut milk, all the teaching about the countryside, the foraging, cooking and copper-potting, were just dreams. No gathering of ingredients together, under the long, green, slime fronds. No passing on of powers. She allowed herself a wry smile – no six-fingered hands, anyway.

"I am knowing what has been happening, my Dears," Hobnail whispered eventually, her eye blinking with realisation. "This be's the work of Crow-cus!" Warty Toad and Snidey Slug looked at each other, puzzled. "Crow-cus, the Baby-Snatcher."

Ever since Hobnail had heard about the child, she had been concerned that Crow-cus would *find* him and snatch him *away* from her. She thought, if he found out there was a baby in the forest, he would report to the Leaf Man and then be sent on a mission to steal him. All this time, she had been concerned to keep Kipperling hidden from them, in case the black-winged shadow swooped down and seized her baby-bundle, to carry him off with a triumphant *crauk, crauk!* Hobnail knew how often Crow-cus flew around her tumbledown chimney. There would never have been any hope of keeping this quiet.

However, she had got it *all* wrong. Her inner eye had worked it out. This third eye, which saw what others were thinking, had flashed understanding into her mind. She had got this all the wrong way round! Whilst Snidey Slug and Warty Toad thought they had found the baby in the forest and whilst she was keen to keep him a secret from the Leaf Man, *he knew all the time!* The Leaf Man had set this up. Liar-nel had hatched a devious plan to get her into trouble! He had *arranged* to drop the little one in the undergrowth, just waiting to be found. He had *wanted* her Dear Ones to hurry-scurry back to her and tell her of his little, wet baby-face. And who should he ask to assist him? The answer was obvious, now. Crow-cus!

The Leaf Man knew Hobnail would not be able to resist the baby's cries. He knew that if he could trick her into caring for him, he could send trouble her way. Who, in the town, would sympathise with her? They would see only an old hag, with a twisted spine and twelve fingers, disfigured and ugly. They would see only her yellow teeth and her dirty clothes. They would know that she lived in a filthy, weather-worn cottage, right on the edge of town, where no one wanted to go. They would point their fingers and cry, "Baby Stealer!" "Child Thief!" "Kiddy-napper!"

Hobnail looked at her Dear Ones. They were so loyal in their affection for her; so unconditional in their love. She gathered them to her and they nestled in their favourite places, craving comfort. "This is what is being happening," their mistress explained softly. "I is thinking that Little Kipper is being taken by spiteful, nasty fae creatures. You is remembering what changelings is?"

Warty and Snidey nodded. They remembered.

Hobnail continued with her thoughts. "Little Kipper is being a quiet, good Baby-suck-Thumb and in the nights the nasty, spiteful fae creatures is a-callings on him. He so very beautiful and perfect-being, is meaning that's the faeries wants him for themselves and so I thinks he is swapsies with a changeling."

This seemed to make some sense to her pets. They knew about changelings and how a pretty baby could be swapped by the faeries so that they could keep him for themselves, and leave a nasty, bad-tempered faerie in his place – but how did old Crow-cus get the baby, if the fae creatures had him?

"Baby Kipperling faerie-flying through the air in the night is, and then *poom!* he is being dropsied down! Babies is heavy cargo for little faerie winglets. Crow-cus misses no tricks and is finding him, quick-stickery. Baby-Snatcher he be, see.

Crauk! Crauk! I hears him." Hobnail paused to wipe a tear which had pooled on a tired eyelid. "And Liar-nel gets my little, wet baby-face. And he is tricksing me."

Warty Toad understood perfectly now. That was why there had been a baby in the undergrowth. That was why nobody was looking for him. He hadn't even been missed, yet! If the faeries were behind this, there would have been an exchange; a changeling would be in Little Kipper's place and no one would be the wiser. Yet.

In time though, the parents would see that their child was different from before. Their child would be wizened and ugly and surly. They would be looking for an answer – and the fibbing brothers would provide one. They would let it be known that Mistress had taken their real child. They certainly would not tell the truth about the faeries' swap.

The toad turned it all over in his mind. Why though? Why would the Leaf Man want to do this?

Chapter Eight

Hobnail knew dawn was approaching. She sensed the lifting of the night and saw the darkness was giving way to a cold, grey mizzle. She did not have many hours to solve her problem; she had hidden a baby away and she was in a lot of trouble. She knew that Liar-nel would be ready to act and would be relishing the opportunity to make her life difficult. She tipped her Dear Ones into her lap and, in answer to Warty's puzzled expression, hurriedly explained.

"The Leaf Man is being well-named as Liar-nel," she began. "He is of liar in nature and laughs at my expense all the times. He is not liking of me and I is not liking of him."

That much was obvious, the toad thought, but in opening his mouth to ask further, he was shushed gently, through yellow teeth, and told to listen.

Many, many years before, when Hobnail had first entered the green dinge under the long, green, slime fronds, she was an unwelcome visitor. She had strayed that way, one aimless afternoon, an idle fancy of exploration taking her a considerable distance from her home. Unknown to her, messages were passed rapidly through the moss she squelched on, and whisperers were everywhere.

It had not been long before the Leaf Man stood before her, challenging her right to be there. "Trespasser!"

Hobnail had blinked in disbelief. The curious, leafy creature barred her path and, although his greeting was hissed unpleasantly, he grinned as if in friendship. It was as if she amused him and yet, he wished to alarm her. She said not a word in reply, uncertain of how to respond, and merely clenched tight her six-fingered fists.

"We do not tolerate trespassers here," the stranger informed her, still smiling. "This is my domain and you are not welcome." He paused, waiting for her reaction.

Still there was none.

"Nothing to say in reply, my dear?" the Leaf Man queried, thrusting his wide smile closer, noticing Hobnail's hands, hunched shoulders and twisted gait. "Perhaps you should tell me your reason for being in these parts, hmm?" He looked around him. "I'm sure my minions would like to know why your whiskery, frowning face has arrived where it shouldn't, and exactly where those clumsy, great boots are taking you."

Hobnail's good eye narrowed in irritation. How very rude.

Her greyed-out one began to think of a plan to protect her.

Her inner eye woke up and stared secretly at this trickster, trying to read his thoughts.

So many times in her sad life she had been cast out and not wanted. So many times she had had to fight for her right to be herself, in a world that shunned her. She had only just begun to live in the old shepherd's cottage at the edge of the forest; she had only just begun to feel strong and brave. Today, she had only been taking an exploratory walk and did not like to be confronted in this manner. And she was certainly not going to be ordered about by a spiky stick with a false smile and a belligerent attitude. So Hobnail drew herself up as best she could, still a little stooped but darkly determined, and although anxiety knotted her stomach, she spoke quietly, with purpose and dignity. "I has enough spite and nasty-mean peoples in my life. I wills be treading where I wishes to. I wills be collecting whatevers I is needing. I wills do as I is wanting to, thank you very much so."

The place under the long, green, slime fronds was still. All that could be heard was a steady drip,

drop,

dribble,

drobble.

Unfortunately, Hobnail's brave words seemed to have no effect other than to cause some entertainment, for the Leaf Man smiled even more broadly at her and, of all things, *winked.* With a twiggy click of his fingers, the silence between them was broken. A murmuring brewed up in the moss; a steady *clack, clack, clack* began; titters and sniggers echoed around; a large, black crow *crauk-crauked* overhead. Hobnail began to feel uncomfortably out-numbered. The Leaf Man still barred her path.

"My, my! You show spirit! But, little crone, are you *really* ready to spar with *me*?" His smile never faltered. It stretched from left leaf-ear to right leaf-ear and he put his head on one side as if waiting for an answer. None was forthcoming. "Nothing more to say? Ah, but forgive me. I'm sure you are wondering who I am, so allow me to introduce myself. My name is Liar-nel." There was a pause. "And this green, secret place, is my territory." He gestured around him with an airy wave of a hand, taking no notice of Hobnail's obvious unease. "Whichever way you look at it, Petal, you are surrounded, so what are you going to do, my little hunched-up, disagreeable friend? Where will you run?"

Hobnail took time to listen to her third eye. *Do not trust the smile*, it told her. *He plans to befuddle you. He will tell you no truth and will try to send you wrong ways.* Her greyed-out eye helped her to think carefully and plan her next move, for move she must. There was little point standing there under the long, green, slime fronds, feeling foolish.

Realising that she would have to behave differently, she spoke at last, trying to sound polite. "I is looking for a ways out, Leaf Man. I seems to have waylaid myself and I needs home for rest feeling, if you please so."

"Well, well, that's better," came the reply. "Manners at last! Many have wandered here and got lost. Many have been sucked down into the depths of green, slime pools, never to be seen again. You, my Sweet, are lucky to have found me! The way out is, obviously, the reverse of the way you came in. Look over there. I will show you the way out." So saying, Liar-nel pointed in the direction of a dark, overgrown path, barely noticeable through the dinge. "You must promise not to return, though."

Hobnail knew she hadn't come down that path. She knew this was a trick. Where would that path lead her? She had no desire to find dangerous slime pools, or to get lost in this strange place. Her eye of reason and thinking, of plotting and planning, warned her to be careful. She must not antagonize this scoundrel. She must move cautiously, with thought, and keep her wits about her. She must act as if she were grateful. She must pretend to go along with his little game, if she were to reach home safely.

"I is thankful of your helpfulness," she murmured, looking down at the mossy ground, promising nothing. "I thinks I will be home going now."

Two twiggy creatures poked their heads out of their snug, leafy cocoons and giggled. One was nestled at Liar-nel's feet and the other swung from a trailing twine attached to his wrist. Both were grinning, thoroughly enjoying the situation that was playing out before them.

"Off you go, then!"

Snigger.

"That's the way!"

Titter.

"Just down that pretty path!"

Chortle.

"Bye-bye!"

Of course, the path had *not* been the right one, just as Hobnail had suspected. She had to hide for long, miserable hours until she could make her way back, under the cover of darkness. By the time she reached home, she felt wretched with tiredness and unease. She was certain that Liar-nel had known her every move – after all, he had his informers – and it annoyed her to think that he felt he had taught her a lesson. She felt humiliated and cross, determined not to let him get the better of her. How dare he tell her where she could and could not go?

From that first meeting on, Hobnail decided to ignore the warnings of the Leaf Man and had gathered her courage together in her twelve-fingered fists, making her way under the long, green, slime fronds, regularly. Of course, she did so with great care, always aware of spies and gossips, but her gathering trips were of such value to her, that it was always worth the risk. Little by little, she learnt to find her way. Little by little, she grew bolder. Little by little, she annoyed Liar-nel more and more.

How dare she keep entering his secret world without his permission?

He wanted to know everything about her; who she was with and what she did. He wanted to know when she arrived at Great Boulder and when she left. He wanted an opportunity to punish this persistent intruder, who collected and squirreled away odd items for strange activities in the Dark Hole.

He wanted to be rid of her.

He watched and waited.

"So he's just being mean?" squawked Snidey Slug, quite indignant.

"Mean-nasty-spitefuls he's being."

"That's why he wants to get you into trouble with your little Poppet," commented Warty Toad.

"He is wanting mores than that, my Dears. He is wanting me in cold, dark prison-jail-dungeon place, flung, and I is not going!"

There was no more time for explanations. As the two Dear Ones knew already, they had to find out where little Kipper lived and who he belonged to. Before long, the people in the town would realise the change in their child's looks and behaviour, and Fiblet and Fibkin would be spreading their lies.

Clapping her hands together in sudden resolve, Hobnail dispatched her Dear Ones to the town. They were told to be fearless and unflinching. They would have to creep down the track, slide and hop through tree roots and leaves, avoiding nettles and brambles. They would have to follow the dug-in grooves, squeezing along the ruts and hollows. They would have to make their way down the wobbly lane to the pot-hole-peppered, tarmac road. They would have to keep their eyes open. They would have to listen for news at doors and windows. They would have to watch out for big boys with sticks, curious cats with quick claws and demon dogs with deadly teeth. They would have to look out for each other. And report back to their mistress.

She had to know where her tiny joy-bundle came from.

"How long should we give her, Liar-nel?"

"Not as long as she needs."

"Should we start to spread the word, Liar-nel?"

"Soon, little leaflettes. Soon."

There was one last thing for Hobnail to do, before jumping on her trusty bicycle, returning to the seashore and wading to her sea-cave to retrieve Baby-suck-Thumb. She wanted a charm. For all her abilities with her greyed-out plotting eye and her thought-reading, future-looking eye, she still needed luck on her side. She *did* have a plan, and she *did* know what the Leaf Man was doing, but she needed a little comfort that all would be well.

The long, green slime fronds began to glow in the first light of the morning. They dripped and

dropped and

dribbled and

drobbled

onto her head, as she made her way to the Dark Hole.

Great Boulder was in no mood to be rushed. It mumbled and grumbled when the stone was tapped on its knobbly surface to awaken it.

"Great Boulder, do not be making of grumbelacious noises now, for goodness sakes of graciousness!" Hobnail hissed. "I is having secrets of very important natures and you must be of assistance to me. Be not you forgetting I have my barb about me!"

Without further complaint, and more than a little perturbed, Great Boulder rocked forwards and backwards, rumbling only a little, until the Dark Hole could be accessed.

Feeling her way over the stones, not wishing to use any light, Hobnail found what she was looking for. There, safely nestling on a ledge of the Forbidden Wall, was the little jar which housed the gold and turquoise butterfly. Her wings still shimmered faintly, even though she had long since been crushed.

Hobnail allowed herself a small moment of sentiment. A tiny tear welled in her working eye "My poor broken sister," she murmured. "We are more the sames being than you is knowing. Both of us is damaged beyond repair-making. We must be staying together as no ones is wanting us likes we be."

Then, shaking her head quickly to force away the self-pity, Hobnail ripped part of the wing and shaped it into an oval, her twelve-fingered hands, skilful and swift. The remainder was returned to the jar as, smiling to herself, she reached for a book from the top shelf. Her idea would be both pretty *and* bring her good fortune! The book was not actually a book at all, for inside the front cover was a cut out section, acting as a secret box. There, still wrapped in a fine veil of cobwebs, was a gold locket which Hobnail had kept all her life. She had stolen it as a scolded child, hoping it might one day buy her freedom from the cruelty she endured. It hadn't done because she had grown fond of it and was convinced that it gave her good luck. She had become superstitious about its charm and now knew that it would be the perfect case to hold her gold and turquoise butterfly wing. The perfect talisman. Her 'Sister'.

Hobnail hung it around her stringy neck and tucked it under her overcoat, feeling it warm against her wizened chest. She felt stronger now.

However, Warty Toad and Snidey Slug were *not* feeling particularly strong. They were not feeling brave, or heroic, or bold. Despite their instructions, they felt neither fearless, nor unflinching. In fact they felt very fear*ful* and indeed, flinched at even the slightest sound, as they plopped and slid their way to the town. They had a bad case of the eebie-jeebies.

What if there *were* big boys, curious cats and demon dogs? What would they do to escape?

And there were so many houses in the town. How could a small slug and a rather plump toad visit them all?

The task seemed impossible. Feeling both hopeless and helpless, the two made their way as best they could toward the houses. The sky had lightened but hung drab and grey. It suited their mood. They were nearing the wobbly lane now and knew that soon they would be in the open, unable to take cover on the tarmac road.

It was just as Warty was seriously considering a change of plan, that they felt a slight fluttering overhead. Suddenly cautious and somewhat jittery, both toad and slug froze, hoping the hedgerow would offer them enough shadow to be hidden. There was another flutter and then an audible sigh.

"We can't find him! We can't find him!" a tiny voice tinkled. "We're in so much trouble with Old Grandmother! We must go right back to the beginning and search again. Right back to the ugly changeling. Why didn't the magic dust work? How *could* we have dropped him?"

Snidey Slug's eyes popped out on their stalks as, quickly, he risked a glance upwards. There on a prickly branch of hawthorn, sat two, dejected fae creatures, wings quivering with exhaustion. Both Warty and Snidey dared hardly breathe. They had to listen carefully and keep their wits about them.

"Crow-cus might have got him. He watches so carefully."

"Then we won't be able to get him back!"

"He might still be in the forest somewhere. We've searched from the Turrets to here, already. We can't keep going backwards and forwards."

There was a tinkling sound as faerie tears began to fall and then a sudden flutter, and they were gone.

Warty Toad looked at Snidey Slug. Snidey Slug looked at Warty Toad. They had done well. They had crept along without being caught by boys, cats or dogs. They had kept alert and listened.

So the fae creatures *had* dropped little Poppet after a changeling swap, on the orders of their Old Grandmother. And now, the two companions knew which house he had been taken from.

They made haste back to the tumbledown cottage to tell Hobnail what they had learned.

Chapter Nine

It was just as Hobnail was packing a bottle of fresh hazelnut milk into her bicycle basket, that her two Dear Ones hopped and plopped and slithered and slothered, breathlessly to her side. As quickly as they could get their words out, they told their mistress what they had discovered. She knew the house with the turrets well.

"You is clever being, my precious pets," she breathed in relief at the news, tucking her hair inside her netted hat and adjusting the pirate patch over her eye. "I is knowing of the house with the poky turretations and I wills be taking Baby-suck-Thumb backs to his place of belonging." Darkness shadowed her face for a moment and there was a warning tone to her voice. "They's better be's looking after him with more carefulness in future moments. I is not taking him homes twice-times."

Warty Toad and Snidey Slug understood perfectly. To lose a baby once to the faeries was unfortunate. To do it twice would be careless indeed. They knew that Hobnail would keep the baby if she thought she could possibly get away with it; Little Kipper's parents would not have a second chance.

"Dear Ones," she continued, "you must be hiding of yourselves, if you please so. Liar-nel and his two foliage friends will be outs and abouts and I has no space in my minds for worry-being abouts you both. Takes yourselves to the Dark Hole and be staying withins, for my return-coming."

The two pets were keen to do as they were told. They still felt nervous after their last run-in with Fiblet and Fibkin, and neither of them wanted to be frightened again. The thought of the welcoming Dark Hole gave them comfort and, after receiving a fond pat and a stroke, they set off to hide. They would have to take care if they were to reach the Dark Hole without being spotted, but they knew many different routes and so, could change their course if necessary. Besides, they reasoned, the Leaf Man and his minions would be far too interested in what their mistress was doing, to take much notice of a fat toad and dull, grey slug, even if they *did* belong to her.

Little chirruping sobs, like that of a baby bird, greeted Hobnail as she paddled her way into the sea-cave. The baby had woken up and, whilst he had been amused by the dangling seashells for a short while, and soothed by the rhythm of the waves against the rocks below, hunger now consumed him.

"Shush, shush my pipsy-popsicle! I has your milky-nut drink here. Be nots upset, baby-pie!"

So saying, Hobnail took the crying bundle from the shelf where he had been left and peered at his creased-up, little face. Relief and recognition washed over him. His sudden smile filled her with a warm glow, as if the sun had come out.

"We is journeying on my wheel-cycle, chip-choppery, my little one," Hobnail told her charge, offering him the bottle of milk, which he sucked at, greedily. "You must be of gentle quietness, in my basket. I's will wrap you bundle-tight, to safe keeps you, but you must be hush-a-bye-baby being. I wills takes you homeward."

The rusty bicycle was waiting for them both on the cliff top, hidden against a gorse bush. The nearby sheep took no notice, as usual, continuing to munch the salty, windswept grass as the hunched, odd figure, carrying a woollen bundle hurried past. With a whiskery kiss planted on his forehead, tucked up tightly as he was, and snoozing away a warm, milk-filled tummy, Kipperling made no noise. Two black boots pushed hard down on the pedals and soon the wind was blowing through Hobnail's damson hair. Despite the urgency of her mission and the apprehension of what lay ahead, she couldn't help but feel the usual exhilaration of travelling at speed: the whizzing rush of air downhill, the burn in her legs on the incline. She didn't notice the brambles whipping her face or the nettle stings at her ankles. She whooped with excitement and determination. She had a job to do; a *vital* job to do. The odds were stacked against her, but she would not fail her Baby-suck-Thumb!

"You sees me, Liar-nel!" she yelled up to the sky. "You won'ts be getting the betters of me!"

Great Boulder was not happy to be ordered about by anyone other than Hobnail, least of all a self-important toad and a smug slug, and certainly never twice in the same day. It grumbled more than usual when asked to roll away from the entrance to the Dark Hole, and its rumblings echoed through the dinge. It flatly refused to cooperate and there was a great risk it would send a moaning message to all the watchers and listeners around. Warty made a mental note to let Hobnail know about its behaviour and was already looking forward to the spike which would inevitably follow. Fortunately, before too much fuss had been made, he spotted a small gap as Great Boulder had not closed up properly from before, and he and Snidey Slug could just about squeeze through. They landed in a heap, on the ground, in the dark.

"Can we have a light on, do you think?" asked Snidey, a rather small voice in the gloom.

"Why?"

"I – I'd rather see everything in its place," he replied, a little hesitantly, "and then we can settle and wait."

"See everything in its place?" queried Warty. "What *do* you mean? What do you *think's* happened to everything? No one can get in here – Great Boulder wouldn't let them!"

"It's just that I – I – I think I'd feel better, that's all," faltered Snidey, a pale pink colour rising in his cheeks.

Warty Toad snorted with laughter. "You're *scared*, aren't you?" he gurgled, his fat throat wobbling and gulping in amusement. "Who's a scaredy-slug? Scaredy Snidey Slug!"

Snidey pursed his wet lips in a silent sulk and slithered off in the direction of the Forbidden Wall. He would not give Warty Toad the satisfaction of knowing how he felt; he would not rise to the bait. Slithering his way up the ledges of the wall, it wasn't long before he found the glass bottles of glow worms and, one by one, he wrapped himself around each of the lids. He sent a little nervous tremble through his soft body, by forcing himself to think about Fiblet and Fibkin, and so the jars were shaken gently. The glow worms awoke and a faint glimmer shone from them. The Dark Hole was filled with a shifting luminosity which cast shadows on the other walls and made Warty Toad look as if he were a weird reflection in a bendy mirror. He was not a pretty sight.

It was just as Snidey was about to descend to the ground once more, when a certain jar caught his eye. Rainbow colours shone from it, ever-changing in the glow worms' light. They flashed and sparkled, shimmering and glistening. For a second or two, the slug stopped, transfixed. Whatever *was* this? Whatever was this thing of *real* beauty? This heavenly, hypnotic kaleidoscope of colour? He gazed at the jar, eyes bamboozled and mouth open, utterly mesmerised for a moment. Then, slowly, it dawned on him. Of course! Hobnail's precious gold and turquoise butterfly bits!

The slug glanced down at Warty Toad on the ground below. A snidey smile began to spread upon his previously sulky face…

The bicycle bounced in the puddles of the lane, brown splashings licking Hobnail's boots as she peddled towards the town. The hedgerows had not disappointed her and so she had been able to gather a hasty handful of hemlock and a pretty posy of periwinkle on the way. Otherwise she had not stopped. The hemlock was stuffed safely up one sleeve and remembering her Great Aunt Tabitha's words: "Know your poisons!" she had taken care to wash her hands in a ditch. The periwinkle, gathered at just the perfect age of the moon that month, had been popped under her hat. She was pleased that the sky was thick with cloud, as soon she would have to take cover and wait for it to become dark. Moonlight would not be her friend tonight. She had to be sure that all lights had winked, then blinked, then closed their eyes, for her to creep along, undetected. She knew of a secret corner tucked behind the wall which surrounded Ivy Turrets. She and Baby-suck-Thumb could cuddle together, hidden in the undergrowth, until the time was right. Her bicycle would have to be concealed, also. Hobnail remembered a hawthorn bush nearby. Nobody would look in that! Perfect.

Slowing down and keeping her head bowed so any passing person would see only a black, netted hat, she located the hawthorn and wall with ease. Hiding places were essential to her and she had many, dotted around the town. Silently, the bicycle was propped up inside the bush and Hobnail took Baby-Bundle from his basket. Looking left and right to check all was clear, the two then hid themselves round the corner of the wall, one with knees drawn up, the other with thumb securely in mouth.

And so Hobnail waited.

And waited.

And waited.

After a while, it became harder and harder to see the detail of her secret den as the light dimmed. No longer could she make out each individual crack in the stonework of the wall. The clinging ivy seemed to be one dark mass now, and although she could hear tiny scrapings of beetles, she could not see where they were. Whenever a spider ran over her hand, she felt the feathery scuttering, but did not know or care how big it was, as she sat patiently biding her time in the growing nightfall.

Eventually, feeling rather numb, Hobnail stretched out one great boot, hearing her old knee click as she did so. She tutted softly and rubbed her hairy leg, stiffly creaking to her feet. The perimeter wall was high, so she left Little Kipper amongst the leaves and scrabbled to get a foothold. One stone at a time, gripping here and grasping there, Hobnail managed to climb up enough to take a peep over the top. She could see the tips of the turrets and the three tall chimneys of this grand house, moodily silhouetted against the night sky. Only one turret window was lit, the others already asleep. It would not be long now.

Hobnail returned to her hiding place and waited.

"Are you hungry, Warty?" queried Snidey Slug, trying to sound as innocent as possible. Warty Toad looked at the slug, suspiciously.

"A bit, I s'pose," he replied. "Why?"

Snidey slithered down from the Forbidden Wall, his plan making him twitch his mouth in amusement. He joined the toad on the ground of the Dark Hole, patting his tummy and belching a little as if he had had a large meal.

"Gosh, I'm not," Snidey declared. "I've just been eating some stray beetles and gritty worms on a shelf up there and they were *de-lish*!"

Warty Toad looked surprised at this. He thought that Snidey's favourite food was tender leaves, gently steamed, or perhaps soaked in a bit of mouse or squirrel stew gravy. Gritty worms and beetles were *Warty's* staple diet. How odd! He regarded his little friend, warily. "I'm not sure I altogether believe you, Snidey," he countered. "Why were beetles and worms on the loose up there? Mistress doesn't let anything out." Snidey Slug drew himself up, importantly. "Ways and means, my Toady Pal. Ways and means."

Warty Toad was astonished. Whatever was the slug talking about? Beetles and gritty worms? On the ledges of the Forbidden Wall? Just there for the taking? It sounded highly unlikely to him. And why on earth was Snidey calling him: "Toady Pal"? He'd never called him that before. It all sounded most peculiar. Warty Toad decided to treat this information with a great deal of caution. "So, Snidey, these beetles and worms," Warty Toad questioned. "You say: 'ways and means'. Which 'ways' exactly? And which 'means'? In short, what are you up to?"

Snidey knew he had Warty's interest now. He had his full attention. With a yawn of pretence and an air of nonchalance, the slug explained that whilst he had been waking up the glow worms, he had noticed the wriggling of something in the dark. To his delight, he realised that there were gritty worms and beetles on the ledges and he had taken his fill.

"But you don't like that sort of food!"

"I do now."

Warty Toad's tummy began to rumble. It had been far too long since he had had a meal and, with all the excitement, he suddenly realised that he had worked up quite an appetite. He glowered at Snidey Slug, who was now rubbing his own belly with a satisfied look and a very smug smile. "I can't get up the Forbidden Wall," stated Warty. "The ledges are too narrow for…"

"Your fat girth?"

Warty Toad frowned. "My webbed feet, actually."

"Do you have webbed feet?" questioned Snidey. "Thought that was just frogs."

Warty made no further comment. Snidey sidled up to him.

"Would you like me to get you something to eat, Warty?"

The sign on the gate was not welcoming. The large print left nobody in any doubt, and Hobnail was not at all happy about having to 'BEWARE' because of the 'DEADLY DANGEROUS DOG!' In addition, the padlock was strong and would not give way easily. The wall was too high to scale, even if you had both hands free, and to attempt it whilst carrying a baby would be impossible. It was not going to be easy to gain access to Ivy Turrets, even though she had waited for all the lights to be out.

She looked up at the house through the spiky metalwork of the gate. Without doubt, all was quiet. Without doubt everyone was sleeping. Perhaps the Deadly Dangerous Dog was, also? There was no time to waste in hesitation, she decided. There was an important job to do. If she failed at this, her first hurdle, little Baby-suck-Thumb would not be returned happily and she would be accused of stealing him. She would be thrown into prison and not see the light of dawn or the stars at night, again. She would not be able to collect under the long, green slime fronds and she would not be able to ride her bicycle to the cliffs. She would not be able to have fun under Great Boulder and she would never be able to visit her sea-cave again.

And what of Warty Toad and Snidey Slug? What would they do without her?

Hobnail thought of her Dear Ones hiding in the Dark Hole, sick with fright, behaving beautifully, waiting like good, little pets, for her safe return. She could not fail them.

A dreamy, creamy, willo-the-wispy, flowery, melty-in-the-mouthy, rainbow sparkly essence filled Warty Toad's mouth. He drooled as he swallowed its delicious, sweet, honeysuckle-tissue gorgeousness. Ohhhhhhh wow. Ohhhh wow. Mmmmm…. Yummy. Yummy. Yummy. In. His. Tummy.

He kept his eyes tight shut, just as Snidey had told him to, so he could savour the flavour. Worms had never tasted this good.

The old shawl made a perfect papoose for Little Kipper. He was bundled up tightly against Hobnail's chest, enabling her two six-fingered hands to be free. She allowed herself a moment to look at his soft eyelashes and his downy blonde hair, as he slept. So beautiful! No wonder the faeries had wanted him. They always wanted the blonde ones.

A strange feeling of pins and needles began in her fingers. In her extra fingers. They began to buzz and crackle and burn – hot, hot. They glowed bright white and lit up Hobnail's face as if she held children's firework sparklers. With a triumphant smile, she took hold of the padlock and zapped her fizzing fingers into each side.

CLANG!

The padlock fell to the ground and the huge gate swung open before her.

Chapter Ten

Once the fizzing of the padlock had ceased and all was still apart from the distant hooting of an owl, Hobnail entered the private grounds of the grand residence. The driveway was lined with tall poplar trees, harsh and soldier-straight, leading the way to the front door. A tarnished lantern swung in the slight breeze, casting shadows over the stone steps, creaking on its rusty hook. Ivy clung to the walls and spread its fingers up the turrets, which were silent and dark. It was not at all a hospitable place at this time of night. No doubt, in the summer, the flowers and sunshine would make the house look warm – welcoming, even – but at this hour, only the bats in the turrets were happy.

Drawing Little Kipper's papoose closer to her with one arm, Hobnail tiptoed from poplar to poplar, keeping as hidden as she could, in case someone looked out of a window. Her blind eye was working hard, plotting and planning, as the scene before her unfolded and information was gathered from her good eye. Was there a side door? Was there a window? Were there some cellar steps outside, where she could gain access? Her inner eye was silent. She found it too difficult to see what people were thinking when she did not know who or where they were. She could not tell what was going to happen either; this was all unknown territory to Hobnail and she had to concentrate on keeping her Poppet safe. Her Sister talisman felt warm against her bony chest, giving her courage. And so, two scruffy black boots made their way almost to the front door and then veered off to the right, to creep around the side of the great house.

Two leafy sticks, with secret smiles, already on the stone steps, went unnoticed.

"Warty Toad?"

"Mmmm…"

"Warty Toad, you are dribbling."

"Mmmm… mmm."

"Warty, do you know what you have been eating?"

Silence.

"You're going to be in soooo much trouble!"

Two amber eyes stared at Hobnail. She stopped in her tracks and stared back.

There was a sudden *hiss-siss!* and a low, threatening *grrrrr-owl*. Then a fluffy, ginger tail disappeared through a cat flap which banged shut.

"So! There *is* being a side door for me to quiet enter by," Hobnail whispered to herself. "I is thanking of you tiny, ginger growler."

The side door proved no obstacle to Hobnail, the lock opening noiselessly at the slightest tap of one electrical finger. Within seconds, she was inside the house, back pressed up against a wall, heart thumping and bumping. Kipperling sensed her apprehension, bundled to her chest as he was, and softly whimpered, but soon he found his little pink thumb and closed his eyes tight shut. Waiting to check for any sound from the occupants, Hobnail tried to steady her breathing. All was silent. All was hushed. No dog, then? She remained on her guard.

The passage leading from the side door opened up into an imposing hall, with doors all around and a wide, carpeted staircase. Hobnail reasoned that the baby's room would be upstairs, possibly next to his parents'. She hoped above all else that the baby's cot would not be in the same room as them. She looked down at her feet. The muddy, black boots would leave their prints on each step, but that wouldn't have to matter. Many people wore such boots; they would not be able to identify her.

Tip-toe. Creak. Pause.

Tip-toe. Creak. Pause.

Tip-toe. Creak. Pause.

How many steps were there? It seemed to take forever to reach the top, one hand clutching the ornamental banister railing and the other cradling her precious bundle. Each riser seemed to have its own unique voice and Hobnail grimaced every time, holding her breath and waiting to listen for movement or murmuring. Her good eye looked ahead, searching for clues. Which of all those doors, with fancy decorations, was the right room? How could she know? She dared not enter without being sure. To add to her discomfort, huge portraits of previous owners glared down at her, disapproving of her trespass, making her feel a wizened, hunched, poor creature in the midst of all this grandeur. She had never been anywhere like this before.

And then, just as she reached the spacious landing, Hobnail noticed a door with a sign. The sign was a picture of a stork with a baby basket hanging from its beak. No additional explanation was necessary. Behind this door was the nursery! One clammy, six-fingered hand clasped the door knob and turned it, slowly.

"You're in for it now," commented Snidey Slug, from a safe position on a ledge as far away from Warty as he could get. "Fancy eating *that!* Of all things! Tut, tut."

Warty Toad felt suddenly sick. The dreamy, creamy, willo-the-wispy, flowery, melty-in-the-mouthy, rainbow sparkly essence had evaporated. Its delicious, sweet, honeysuckle-tissue gorgeousness had been replaced with bitter bile as he swallowed and gulped, realising what he had done. He couldn't even speak.

"You just *didn't* think, did you?" continued Snidey. "You just went ahead and opened your mouth and whoops-a-daisy, look what dropped in!"

Warty looked over to the Forbidden Wall, in misery. The empty gold and turquoise butterfly jar lay empty, on one side. There were no signs of gritty worms on the loose, or black beetles scurrying about. It had been a rotten trick. How could he have fallen for it?

"Oops," Snidey called over softly.

The door opened into a cosy room, warmed by the fire which was still burning in the grate. A single person's bed was against one wall, but no one slept in it. Perhaps it had been for a nanny; perhaps she had fled, frightened by the change in the child she had been caring for.

"Goodness lucks it is for me that the bed is empty being," thought Hobnail to herself as she entered.

A Moses basket, with lambswool blankets had been set at the foot of the bed, but it too was empty. Hobnail sighed when she saw it. This then, was the moment. She folded back a corner of the snug shawl which had been such a perfect papoose for her Baby-suck-Thumb and gazed at his sleeping face. "You is having the face of the angels, my sweet popsicle," she whispered. "I wills always be lovings of you. I wills always be wantings of you. Comes to me in my cottage tumble place, or in my sea-cave, or evens the Dark Hole and I wills be waitings for you, if you is needings of me."

A last, lingering kiss was planted on his forehead, before the baby was tucked up in the basket, sleeping peacefully, a gentle smile pouching his soft cheeks. Hobnail then pulled the pretty periwinkle from under her hat and laid it on the pillow of the single bed. It would help heal the bad memories of changelings and keep happy memories of Little Kipper, only.

Dear little poppet.

But that was not the end of Hobnail's work that night. She let the papoose fall to the floor and touched Sister to give

her strength. She had to face the changeling. She had to deal with fae creatures' magic. This would be the scary part.

A cold wind lifted two twiglets further up the steps, to the front door. They clattered against it and then stood upright.

"Do you think we should knock at this rather magnificent door, Fibkin?"

"Whatever do you mean, Fiblet? We wouldn't want to wake everyone up, now, would we?"

"No! That would be a simply *terrible* idea."

Knock. Clatter. Knock.

A few steps on the left hand side of the nursery room caught Hobnail's eye. They seemed to lead into one of the turrets. She clenched her fists together and braced herself. This must be where the changeling lay. This must be the room that her baby-pie once had. The rooms were connected, after all. She had to be right.

As Hobnail put one black boot on the first step, there was a distant sound. It was a faint tapping. Then it came again, louder this time. A sort of a knock. And then a sort of a clatter.

And another knock, again a bit louder. It came from downstairs. It came from the front door. Knock! Clatter! Knock!

No time to lose, then.

Hobnail trod the steps quickly, less wary of her own noise, opened the turret door and within seconds, she faced a baby's cot.

It was not a pretty cot.

It was solidly built, with strong bars making it look more like a cage than a cradle. A heavy, snoring breathing was coming from it. A rasping sort of rattle. A mucous sort of gargle. It was certainly not the sound of sweet, baby sleep. Creeping cautiously now, Hobnail approached. Her blind eye plotted and planned. There must be no hitch. No mistake. No error. She tried to block out the sound of the snoring – and the clattering at the front door. She had to concentrate and use all her knowledge of changelings, even if she risked being caught herself. She peered over the top of the cot.

The creature was not asleep.

It was not a boy. Nor was it a girl.

Its black eyes regarded her coldly. Its foul breath hit her in the face and made her gag. Its skin was wrinkled, and the flesh on its jaw was thin and stretched, clearly outlining the bone beneath. It was grey in colour. The hair on its head was sparse, coarse and knotted. Its nose was sharp and plugged with green snot. Its mouth hung open slightly as it made its grating sound and there were several teeth, sharp and triangular, spread across its dark red gums.

Hobnail had never seen anything so repulsive in all her life. The thing was hideous. Without doubt, this was a changeling of the highest order. It had to be an ancient faerie, possibly an olden queen, who had chosen to live her life in comfort, with this wretched family, forcing them to coddle her and be her servants. Perhaps the Old Grandmother faerie had taken her place.

Hobnail had to be brave. She had to show courage if she were to protect Baby-suck-Thumb and get out of this house. Summoning up as much strength from Sister as she could, she reached inside the cot. Her hands trembled as she did so.

With a sudden *grab!* the changeling shot out two fists and clawed at Hobnail's face, tangling its shrivelled fingers in the net of her hat. Hobnail pulled back in alarm, her hat falling off into its clutches. Screeching like a demon, the changeling lunged at Hobnail's hair and yanked down hard, ripping a strand from her head. Pain seared through her scalp, making her scream out as hot tears welled in her pirate patch. The knocking and clattering downstairs became a bashing and a pounding, as if the house itself was fighting a furious battle. There were sudden shouts and the heavy thudding of feet. Little Kipper, next door, began to wail in distress at the cacophony. Then, just as Hobnail managed to tear herself away from the changeling's clutches, the turret door was flung open with a loud *bang!*

In bounded the Deadly Dangerous Dog.

And his owners.

Guffawing with laughter, two twiggy sticks fell down the stone steps, rolling over and over in the wind which caught them, making them giddier and sillier than ever.

"Sounds like we might have disturbed the people of the house, Fibkin!"

"Oh dearie me. We *never* meant to do that, did we, Fiblet?"

"Never!"

"I rather think *someone* might be caught in the act, so to speak."

"*Really?* Shocking, isn't it?"

And holding leafy hands, they scuttled off towards the forest to tell the Leaf Man of their success.

Hobnail was stuck. She was stuck between a mad, barking Deadly Dangerous Dog, only *just* being restrained by his owners, and an inhuman changeling which seemed to sense her plans. The dog slathered and strained at the collar, baring his teeth in a fearsome snarl, the whites of his eyes showing, trying his best to get at her. The changeling hissed and spat and shrieked and clawed at its cage, gnarled hands stretching to grip and pinch. The two people who had flung open the door looked shocked and pale, their mouths agape at the sight of a hunched, old crone in their child's room and recoiling at the vicious nature of the changeling's attack.

"WHO ARE YOU?" yelled the man in fright and anger. "WHAT ARE YOU DOING IN HERE? WHAT'S GOING ON?"

The woman at his side could not speak. Her eyes were wide in fright and her hands were flat against her cheeks. Neither could believe what they were seeing and hearing.

Hobnail darted a glance past them, to the door. There was no way she could reach it without being caught. A hot wave of panic rose in her as she clasped Sister. The only thing she could think of doing, would be to make a lunge for the changeling, hoping that the people, being terrified of the creature, would back off and let her through. She turned to face the dreadful sight once more, steeling herself for the next onslaught, but – there was an unexpected *flash!*

In an instant, the changeling had become a bright, fae light. Quite without warning, it had changed its form and now, a fiery brightness dazzled and stung their eyes as it proceeded to zip around the room. It scorched the curtains and burned whorls into the walls, pin-wheeling and sparking its way, high up to the ceiling and down, low to the floor. It dived at the man and the woman, intending to wound them, char them and singe them, so they huddled together, their dog whining and cowering at the smell of magic which choked them. It pinged and whizzed and catapulted. It left a trail of bright colour imprinted in the air.

Hobnail froze to the spot.

She watched. She waited.

This needed an experienced hand, dexterity and a keen eye. She knew she had all of these. Her nostrils flared in anticipation of the strike. If she could *just* concentrate as if she were under the long, green, slime fronds... Slowly, she stretched out her arms at either side, twelve distorted fingers spread expectantly, her mouth clamped tight shut.

The changeling bounced from wall to wall like a bluebottle against a window, never quite landing, never quite settling to be caught.

Hobnail watched.

Hobnail waited.

For a millisecond too long, the changeling hovered, teasingly, above her head. Suddenly one of her outstretched arms punched up in the air – and made a *SNATCH!*

She had it!

Hobnail's fist was clenched tightly over her prize. Her hand blistered immediately with the intense heat, but she did not let go. A slow smile spread wickedly across her face and the room glowed yellow as her good eye lit up. Her hips did a little dance. As easy as catching gold and turquoise butterflies!

Then, without further hesitation, she ran. She ran straight past the frightened people and the trembling dog, through the turret door and down the steps into the bedroom, next door. The fire was still burning in the grate. Her greyed-out blinded eye knew only too well what she should do. Risking the dreaded hot coals, Hobnail flung the changeling into the blaze and grasped a poker from the hearth. She jabbed and jabbed to keep the fae light in the flames, recoiling in disgust as it became once more the withered, changeling child reaching out to her with desperate, melting fingers until – with an ear-splitting *screeeeeech!* it flew up the chimney.

All that remained were the sounds of little Poppet's pitiful cries and Hobnail's panting breaths. Her heart hammered in her chest and her legs felt as if they were about to give way – until the Deadly Dangerous Dog appeared at the turret door, once more.

With a swift kiss blown in Kipperling's direction, Hobnail left him. She left him in his Moses basket, in the room where he belonged. And fled.

Chapter Eleven

T he sound of the changeling's screams was still ringing in her ears as Hobnail slammed shut the nursery door, behind her. Perhaps the delay in anyone opening it would buy her enough time to escape from the Deadly Dangerous Dog so she could just make it outside. Perhaps it wouldn't. Clutching Sister and muttering to reassure herself, she pelted past the other doors on the landing until she reached the stairs.

"Chip-choppery! We must quick-hurry, my Sister. Bark-biter runs fast upon our heels and I is not attack-wanting. We must be speed-zooming!"

No worries about the creaks with each step this time! At the sound of the nursery door knob turning though, Hobnail's heart missed a beat. In an instant, she leapt off the stairs and swung herself onto the ornamental banister rail. Legs astride, holding on tight despite the pain in her blistered hand, she slid all the way down, reaching the bottom just as the snarling dog reached the top.

There were shouts of confusion upstairs. Trying to control the mad dog was clearly impossible; he had his quarry in sight and he would not be restrained. So when the people of the house discovered their returned baby in the Moses basket, they left him to the chase. Cries of terror and despair turned to shouts of joy and amazement as the distressed child was swept up into the arms of his parents and smothered with tearful kisses. They neither understood nor cared what had been happening. All that mattered was that their baby was safe once more and given back to them.

Breathless with anxiety and exertion, Hobnail dashed through the great hall at the bottom of the stairs and located the passage to the side door, where she had entered the house not long before. She could hear the Deadly Dangerous Dog panting and slathering behind her and almost feel his breath about her ankles. With a sinking feeling in the pit of her stomach, she realised that she had little chance of escape.

"Greyed-out eye! Sweet Sister!" she cried as she hastened to the exit. "You must be helpings of me, quick-stickery, for I has dog-nippings about me and I is not likings the teeth-bitery of the beast! I is needing a tricksy up my sleeve!"

And then, she remembered. She remembered the hemlock.

She remembered the hemlock, *up her sleeve*.

Hobnail halted with sudden resolution, her boots jarring on the floor. Courageously, she turned upon her assailant and barred his path. She *glowered* at the dog.

"SIT!"

Shocked, the Deadly Dangerous Dog did just that.

"SIT AND STAY!"

Ears back, the Deadly Dangerous Dog sat and stayed.

"You listens to me, horrible hound!" Hobnail ordered. She put one six-fingered hand on the side door's broken lock.

"You wills be sitting and staying in nature. You wills be hush-quiet and not mad-barking-noise-making. I is placing hemlock on this floor, just here, sees you?"

The dog, sat and stayed, watching as Hobnail reached up into her sleeve and pulled out the poisonous plant. He sat and stayed as she laid some stems on the floor between him and the door.

"LEAVE!"

The dog whined and put his great head on his paws, watching warily. He remained absolutely still apart from a slight tremor from nose-end to tail-tip.

"Don'ts you be a-sniffing or a-licking of this, now. You sits. You stays. You leaves."

The dog appeared to understand completely. He was not going to go anywhere near the strange-smelling posy.

"And now," announced Hobnail, brightly. "I leaves also!"

So saying, finally she tugged at the door and disappeared into the night.

Fiblet and Fibkin could hardly contain their excitement as they gurgled and giggled their way to the Leaf Man. They hoppity-skipped through the forest, hand-in-hand, laughing and joking. It had been fun to be picked up by the wind and carried up the stone steps of the grand house. It had been entertaining to throw themselves at the huge front door, making a clatter. It had been exceptionally satisfying to know that they had succeeded in waking up the people and dog, even though there had been a bit of screeching from inside, which contributed. Now surely, Liar-nel would be rid of the peculiar, haggardy-rag-bag who insisted on invading his privacy under the long, green, slime fronds. She should have known he would get the better of her! She should have gone back to wherever she came from and stop her collecting of strange bits and bobs, to squirrel away under that large boulder. She should have left them alone in their green dinge of a world. Served her right. Now she would be caught. Locked up. Key thrown away.

Surely this would mean that she wouldn't be back. Ever. The place under the long, green slime fronds would be all theirs. Alone. The leaflettes couldn't wait to report.

Around the side of the house, two amber eyes stared at Hobnail, once more. There was a flick of a fluffy, ginger tail.

Hobnail gazed back as she pondered her next move.

How tempting!

Here was a truly beautiful cat and at that moment Hobnail knew, without *any* doubt, she needed a cat in her life. Obviously, this needed some serious consideration.

'So far, so good', her eye of plotting and planning seemed to tell her. She had closed the door behind her, leaving the dog paralysed with fear and the people so consumed with delight that she had almost been forgotten. She had found a tap on an outside wall and rinsed her hands of any hemlock traces. She really should not delay any further, however, since her greyed-out eye urged her to leave, as quickly as possible. Hobnail knew this made sense: she should go into the night, silently and swiftly, otherwise it would be very tricky to answer questions and give explanations. She was certainly not going to risk being caught – but there was something about this little creature that excited her. Hobnail was loathe to leave her.

The watchful cat flicked her tail once more.

"You must not be insides going just now, tiny ginger growler," whispered Hobnail. "Is not good timings for kitty-kooties." She looked down the poplar-lined drive to the spiky, metal gate. There was still a fair way to scuttle in the dark, before she would be able to reach her trusty bicycle. She absolutely didn't have any time to chat to cats. "There's hemlock insides the door being – and that nasty snarling-biter is no goods for kitties I is thinking."

The cat continued to stare, unblinking. She had such a pretty, pretty, pink nose.

Hobnail made a decision: it wasn't *stealing*. It was *saving*. It wasn't *theft*. It was *thoughtfulness*.

How could she possibly leave the ginger kitten to live there? With That Dog? And she *had* returned little Kipper, after all. It was a fair swap.

In one swift movement, the cat was scooped up. There was much hissing and spitting, with claws out and fur raised, but Hobnail took no notice. Compared with the changeling's fight of fiendish magic, this little bundle of fluff was nothing.

Snidey Slug had dropped off to sleep. His pursed, pouty mouth issued sweet, whistling noises as he lay curled up on his shelf of safety. He dreamed sluggy dreams of tender roots, shoots and soft spring leaves. Now the glow worm lights were on, he did not have a care in the world.

Warty Toad, on the other hand, was wide awake. He still felt rather queasy and every time he thought about Hobnail, his toady toes became all clammy and moist. He had seen for himself how her spike worked. The words: "Spikes be nastier than sparks!" kept ringing in his ears and made him shudder. Never again would he take pleasure in seeing Great Boulder getting spiked, he thought miserably to himself as he awaited his fate.

The ginger cat did *not* want to go into the bicycle basket. It reminded her of terrifying visits to the vet and so she was wild and scratchy. It had been a struggle for Hobnail to keep hold of the hostile ball of fur as she made her way to the spiky gate, but she had just managed it, and a wash of relief flooded through her when, finally, the grand house was behind her. The bicycle had been retrieved from the hawthorn bush and basket lid opened.

"For goodness sakes of graciousness! This is being for your safe-keepings, little hiss-pot!" exclaimed Hobnail as she tried to stuff the cat inside for the third time. "I is caring for you and this is no times for being nastyful in returns."

The little cat growled.

"You wills be of happy-feeling soon, tiger-lily," Hobnail continued, in a business like tone. "Just in you gets, if you please so."

The little cat flicked out her claws and scratched.

Hobnail cried out and dropped her, scowling in irritation. The cat landed on the ground at her feet and swished her tail. She glared back at Hobnail with determined, golden eyes. It was clear that this adopted pet was going to be quite a handful and far more trouble than a baby. She was spirited and wilful. She was badly behaved and would lash out whenever she wanted to. She was a little imp! Hobnail considered the cat for a moment, head on one side.

She was perfect.

"I is believing there is devilishness of the very devil in you!" Hobnail declared. She paused briefly before announcing: "I shall be calling you 'Lucy-fur'."

Their eyes locked, each neither quite trusting the other. Suspicious. And then, with a slight curl of a set of whiskers as if she understood the joke, and a slight softening of a wrinkled face, there came an understanding between the two of them.

"So the people of the house were alerted?" questioned Liar-nel, extricating himself from his camouflaged, tree hidey-hole. He appeared from the bark of the trunk as if he were being unveiled. It was a graceful, liquid movement which had a mystical quality about it. One moment, he was invisible, the next moment, he was standing in front of them.

"They heard us clattering and knocking at the door," reported Fiblet. "And," he paused, "they had a dog!"

"Even better," smiled Liar-nel.

"And there was a great shouting and barking," added Fibkin. "Anyone would think that they had discovered an intruder!"

Liar-nel took in a deep breath and closed his eyes, better to picture the scene. His leafy robes ruffled as he exhaled in obvious satisfaction. His twiggy fingers wiggled in pleasure. "She did have the baby with her, then? Just like we wanted her to? Did it all go to plan?"

"A baby was squawking loud as loud! Like a smelly, squealing piglet."

"Excellent." The Leaf Man winked at his leaflettes. He knew they had done a good job. Now the nuisance, old Bag-of-Bones would be out of the way. She would not be wandering willy-nilly through his forest, under the long, green slime fronds, with her faithful little friends, anymore. She would be caught and accused of baby-stealing and kiddy-napping. Perfect!

"I think this calls for a celebration, my leafy twiggeries," Liar-nel announced. "Let's have a party! Go and round them all up: Crow-cus, the Moss-makers and don't forget the Mushrumps. We shall make much merriment!"

Fiblet and Fibkin were highly delighted.

The ginger cat was finally in the bicycle basket and the lid firmly secured. There was a feeling of urgency now, as Hobnail knew she had spent enough time close to Ivy Turrets. She longed to be with her Dear Ones under Great Boulder, in the Dark Hole. She felt the need for familiarity of surroundings and wanted to be away from this place. The thought of Warty Toad and Snidey Slug almost brought a tear to her eye. They were *such* good pets! So loyal and trusting. So dependable when the rest of the world seemed against her.

The bent bicycle did not seem keen to move, however. Hobnail was surprised. Usually, it was as ready as she was to whizz, zip, zoom, race and rush. Usually it behaved as if it had a life of its own, willing to speed along the lanes and tracks. *Usually*, all Hobnail had to do would be to climb onto the saddle and push down with her great boots, and she would be away. She cast a worried glance at the wall which surrounded the grand house. She was hidden from view at the moment, but what if the people decided to bring the Deadly Dangerous Dog out of the front gate, whilst she was struggling to get her bicycle moving?

"I has no time for game-playing," she muttered, forcing the wheels to turn. "I must be home in no minutes. Time is sun-dialling fast and soon the dawning will be upon us. Let us be wheel-cycling, if you please so!"

A half turn of a reluctant pedal told her the reason. Hobnail had a puncture. One tyre was deflated, squashed and sad. This was no good at all. Feeling all around the rubber, a large thorn was located with grimy fingers. There was a quiet *psssss!* as the remaining air escaped.

Hobnail tutted to herself. Hiding her bicycle in a hawthorn bush had *not* been the best idea she had ever had. She looked right and left, checking all was clear, before yanking the bicycle onto the road. A poplar tree happened to be next to her. It was as tall and forbidding as the trees on the drive of the grand house had been, but this one seemed to whisper to her, as a slight breeze moved its branches. Hobnail listened intently and then, nodding in thanks, scraped some sap, carefully from its bark. The sticky goo bunged up the puncture hole in her tyre so at least it wouldn't rip on the road home and then it could be pumped up, later. She knew she could not leave the bicycle either here, or at the edge of the forest. Hobnail shuddered at the thought of leaving any clues.

And so, a tired, wizened, old crone slowly made her way past the grand houses; the ones with long driveways and fancy names. She kept to the shadows as she pushed her poor, broken bicycle past the tidy, well-kept houses with clean paintwork and guttering; the pretty bungalows with neatly-striped lawns and flower borders of colour; the welcoming family homes. She winced as it jolted in the potholes of the wobbly lane when the tarmac petered out. Eventually though, she welcomed the ruts and the hollows, because she felt safer. The hedgerows were just beginning to wake up with morning chirrups and rustlings, as she struggled past. The trees on either side bowed to Hobnail in greeting, forming their leafy tunnel, leading her to the tumbledown cottage which was hers. The bicycle was left propped up against a pile of bricks, looking just like it always did. Nobody would know its night time adventure. Gathering Lucy-fur from the battered basket, Hobnail took the short cut then, skirting via the rickety stile along the back of the houses of the town, hidden behind hedgerows and undergrowth, to the forest at last.

Great Boulder rolled over without a grumble when Hobnail finally arrived, sleeping kitten in her arms. It sensed that this cold, damp dawn should welcome the special mistress who appeared, aching and exhausted.

Snidey Slug opened one eye and was the first to speak. Warty Toad was silent.

"All good, Mistress?"

"All is being good, Snidey, my pet."

Snidey looked at the new addition to the family. He wasn't sure what to make of the curious, cradled creature. Warty Toad kept his head well down.

"What's that you've got, Mistress?"

"This is being my new baby-pie, Snidey. Scratchful and growlish is she, but is needing of a welcome home place."

Hobnail settled herself on the rough ground, her head resting against a smooth rock, the worn-out Lucy-fur asleep on her lap. She was almost snoring herself, when Snidey found he could not contain himself any longer.

"Mistress?"

"Yes, Snidey?"

"Warty Toad ate your gold and turquoise butterfly bits!"

Hobnail touched the talisman around her neck. She smiled sleepily, relishing the warmth of her cat hot water bottle.

"I is thinking he would, one days," she replied, calmly. "Be putting out the lights if you please so, Snidey. I is needing some sleep-eye."

Postamble

The long, green, slime fronds never cease their quiet drip,

    drop,

        dribble,

            drobble.

It is almost as if the deep, dark forest has its own clock, dripping away the seconds, minutes, hours, days and nights. The shifting curtain of secrecy continues to droop limpidly over the eerie, hideaway place beneath, keeping the air heavy and moist.

But, the Leaf Man is no longer watching.

The Leaf Man is no longer waiting.

The Leaf Man is no longer listening...

He thinks he is rid of her and is ready to make merry with his minions. He does not know that, as he gathers Crow-cus and the Moss-makers in celebration, she is sleeping under Great Boulder, dreaming of sewing rose petals and catnip into love sachets. He does not know that, soon she will make her way back through the forest to her tumbledown cottage, to continue living her life, with her loyal friends at her side. He does not know that she intends to return, again and again, to the place under the long, green, slime fronds which

    drip and

        drop and

            dribble and

                drobble.

"But are you sure, Mrs. Mushrump?"

"Sure as sure, Mr. Mushrump."

"Are you sure it's not 'hard to say', Mrs. Mushrump?"

"No. It's easy to say. I'm sure as sure, Mr. Mushrump."

"We'll have to tell him, Mrs. Mushrump. We'll have to tell him what you know."

"It'll spoil his party, Mr. Mushrump."

"So are you *sure*, Mrs. Mushrump? Are you *sure* you've seen who you *think* you've seen? Are you *sure* you've heard what you *think* you've heard? It's not just one of your *feelings*, Mrs. Mushrump? Not just one of those *colours* in your head?"

"I'm sure as sure this time, Mr. Mushrump. This is not just a colour-feeling. I *know* who I've seen. I *know* what I've heard. We know something the others don't, for once. It's *easy* to say!"

"It'll be hard to say all this to *him* though, Mrs. Mushrump. It'll be hard to say to *him*. He's not going to be happy."

"You'd best get a move on then, Mr. Mushrump. We're late for the party as it is."